SALT WATER

AND OTHER SHORT STORIES

SEF HUGHES

CONTENTS

MOTHER DEAR

'I know I'm not very good at love.'

Lily made the admission early one Sunday morning as we marched through heavy rain to the cathedral.

'But I would kill anyone who harmed you.'

I stopped dead. She kept on walking past the shuttered greengrocers and Indian restaurants. And soon I was running, trying to catch her, my tears hiding in the raindrops.

————

Her dream: I had grown three times in size, and wings had sprouted from my back. I rose from her arms, up into the air above our town. The streets were filled with people who watched, their mouths and eyes gaping. I spoke to them in a language they didn't understand and ascended further until I was no more than a dim speck. A tiny black star, she said. Then there was a burst of colour and I disappeared. The people went home and nobody spoke of what had happened. Lily ran from door to door, pleading with her neighbours to remember me, but nobody could. When she returned home, my bedroom was empty. There was nothing of me there—the furniture, my bed, my clothes and my pictures had gone, leaving behind no indentations on the carpet or tack marks on the walls. I survived for a while in the corner of her memory—nothing more than a figment—and then she felt me leave that too. She spoke to her sisters about losing something she could not remember, and they scolded her foolishness.

My dream: She couldn't find me. We were in her house and she was young—the age she must have been while I was still a baby. I followed her as she searched the rooms over and over again, speaking, then calling, then shouting my name. Then screaming. I cried and told her that I was there. I begged her to acknowledge me, but she heard nothing. She searched deeper into the house—into rooms that I didn't even remember— down corridors that didn't exist. She moved through the house faster, picking up speed with every step, her volume and pitch increasing until her terror woke me.

Yet, in the half-light of this Castleport day, where clouds settled on the streets, and the crumbling sandstone walls of discount off-licences and betting shops fenced us in, memories of dreams were unreliable and unconvincing. For Lillian Jones, a woman so preoccupied with achieving immortality she barely noticed the existence of her only daughter, the sharing of her dark, subconscious ramblings was a rare moment of weakness and tenderness—one she later retracted. As for me, I kept my dream chained to the inner wall of my skull.

———

Death was Lily's real child. Her favourite. For her, the exit was the most important part of life. Everything else was mere preparation. Like a tiger mother, she hothoused her own demise, doing everything she could to ensure it would excel.

Her strategy was other people. They either liked her or they admired her determination to be liked. There was nothing desperate about it. Quite the opposite— she was hostile. Aggressively good-natured. If Lily discovered you had a problem, she would solve it whether you wanted her to or not. She would bully her way into your life and force her help upon you. With an emotional crowbar, she would pry open your private world and pummel your issues into submission. But, despite her methods and how you felt about your life being molested, it was difficult not to feel grateful after the event. She helped couples clamber back from the brink of bankruptcy and divorce via austerity measures and lifestyle makeovers. She spent hours in hospitals with aged parents of individuals she barely knew to relieve their guilt. She took people into her small home, sheltered and fed them, and helped them get back on their feet, financially and spiritually. She gave her money and time away as if they had no value—but she was buying something.

Her life was punctuated with these displays of guerrilla kindness—often, she'd run several offensives simultaneously. When one of the parishioners broke his leg, she took it upon herself to spend a fortnight nursing him and, having decided this wasn't enough, and despite his protests, she redecorated his house. While fighting on this front, she pushed her charity upon a woman whose husband had just been killed in service, helping her come to terms with her grief by reintroducing her to Jesus. Meanwhile, the uninsured home of a neighbour was burgled and completely emptied. Lily pounced on the opportunity and insisted she stay with us—in my bedroom.

'We can't possibly let a guest sleep on the sofa. You're small. It won't be so uncomfortable for you.'

She then launched an impressive fundraising drive—raffles, a fair, sponsored sporting events, and an auction of donated items—which produced enough money in three weeks to refit the house and pay for several years' worth of insurance cover.

This was typical. I watched as my mother emptied herself of every last drop of kindness. She wrung herself dry for these people.

Which was why, perhaps, there was nothing left for me.

———

Lily rose at five every morning to ensure that the house and her good self were spick and span before embarking on that day's campaign. By the time I woke she'd be gone. My school uniform and breakfast laid out for me. Any money or equipment I needed for that day waiting at the front door. She never got it wrong.

At nine years old, I was the first in school to have my own house key. Just a small piece of brass-coloured metal with a tatty two-tone pink cotton ribbon threaded through the small hole—but it was a powerful object. To the other children it stood for an independence and freedom they had difficulty fathoming, and I revelled in their envy. I'd fake absent-mindedness as I swung it about in the playground, delighting in their jealous glances. After school, however, the key was nothing more than an empty house and a handwritten note with rushed instructions on how to prepare that evening's meal from the ingredients in the fridge.

———

Occasionally, Lily would return before I'd gone to bed. I'd get a:

'How was school, child?'

Or perhaps a:

'What did you learn today?'

But my answers delayed her work, and her eyes were always somewhere else if I chose to respond in detail. When she'd heard enough, she'd make herself a cup of tea and embark on a telephone-based altruistic blitz. Other times, I'd wake up on the sofa to the pain of her poking a finger into my shoulder as she whispered that it was late and I should go to bed.

At weekends, she would wake me at six thirty so I could join her on her quests. I think she found it useful to have me by her side. It meant people could see she wasn't only saving our community from self-destruction, she was doing it as a single mother who had to battle for her and her daughter's survival.

The rules were simple. I was to smile and remain quiet. If spoken to, I had to wait for Lily's signal before responding. And so, I sat in silence in hospital wards, strangers' living rooms, on park benches, in cafés and at unfamiliar kitchen tables. Wherever Lily's charitable warfare took her, I followed behind with a painted-on smile and bored eyes.

————

She went to the cathedral every day, and she did her best to ensure everyone knew it. It provided her with a kind of platform from which she could shape their memories. It gave all her actions a legitimacy as well as a motive. Perhaps it's harder to refuse help from someone who appears to be following a religious calling.

But there was another reason for the cathedral visits. I know this because she had gone over the finer details of her exit strategy with me many times, starting when I was too young to hold the notion of the death of my mother in my head without bursting into tears and begging her to stop. It was to be a performance. Her grand departure was being choreographed in fine detail so she could brand her image onto the collective memory of the community at large. And the production required the services of the bishop. She'd met the Right Reverend Clement Hook at the cathedral the week he was posted there, and elicited his telephone number by claiming to possess an effective cure for a condition she diagnosed by watching him walk towards the pulpit. Over time, she hacked out a place in the man's consciousness and made certain he fully understood her essential role in the community. She worked him well and uncovered several areas of his life that required her expertise—the perfect foundation for a lasting relationship. And 'Clem' eventually agreed that, when the time came, he would offer up her soul at the cathedral.

From the age of eight, I associated this ancient building with her death. She took me there every Sunday. We'd squeeze into an overcrowded pew as close to the altar as we could get—and while the congregation manufactured its droning, oscillating hum of prayers and hymns, I'd imagine myself standing at the front, weeping as I read her eulogy.

'Don't worry about it, child. I've written it down for you. All you have to do is read it out.'

So specific was Lily's planning that, as I grew older, my vision of that inevitable day never changed. As the mourners worked their way through the robotic responses that swept past me and splashed against the altar, I'd hear the heavy footsteps of the pall-bearers as Lily's ample corpse pushed their polished black shoes hard onto the ancient flagstones. I would lift my black veil from my face and turn to look at the oak coffin, generously adorned with brass fittings and floral tributes, and I'd collapse in despair, and the mourners would gasp.

'Poor thing! She's devastated.'

———

Then, on Christmas Eve 1989, she surprised me.

'You have to be careful, child.'

I lifted my face out of a music magazine.

'Hm?'

'I said you have to be careful.'

'What about?'

'You only get one go at life, you know.'

'I know.'

'If you know so bloody much then what is the point of me talking to you? Can you tell me that?'

'Sorry.'

'Do you want me to talk to you or do you want me to shut up?'

'I want you to talk. Sorry.'

'So I should think.'

She was silent for a few minutes while her anger dissolved. I stared into space, not daring to look at her or to return to my magazine in case either were deemed as aggressive, dismissive or both.

She took a sip of port, then, after inhaling sharply through pursed lips, she continued.

'You have to be careful about everything in life, child. You see, everything is about appearance. It is all about how others see you—what they think about you. And at some point soon you are going to have to decide what you want them to think of you. Because...'

The dark red liquid interrupted briefly.

'...it is something that you can control. In fact, you owe it to yourself to control it. And to God, too. Obviously. By being careful, you can make people feel better about themselves. And if you make them feel good about themselves, they feel good about you. Am I making myself clear?'

I nodded even though she wasn't looking to me for a reply. Lily understood, and that was all that mattered.

'Take me. I could be like the rest of them, couldn't I? I could go through life never giving a thought about who I am and what I mean. Most people don't, you know?'

Now she looked at me.

'They do not, trust me. They never give it a second's thought. Cattle. That is what they are. And it is such a waste. Such a shame. And the problem is if you do not think about it, and you do not take action, you just disappear. Nobody knows who you are. Why? Because you do not know who you are. It is not difficult, is it? You do not have to be a genius, do you? But the way people plod through their lives...'

She sighed. She looked at the ceiling. She shook her head. Then she looked at me again.

'...It is as if they are racing to get to the end without touching the sides. Do you know what I mean? It is like they are trying to finish it all as quickly and as painlessly as possible. That's not what the Lord wants, is it? He made this place and all the bad things that are in it so we can go out there and get our hands dirty. Do you understand me, child? This is not a waiting room. This is life. And if you are careful you can make sure it goes on for a long, long time. Long after you are dead, even. Everything we have, the houses, the cars, the clothes, the money, it is all worthless. The only thing that has any value is something we can never actually touch...'

It was dawning on me that this wasn't just another monologue—she was taking the time to tell me about the thing she cared about most. She was actually talking to me. I must be old enough now, I thought. She's starting to see that I'm here. And I was beginning to reel with delight.

'... But we can influence it. Do you know what influence means, child?'

I moved my best concentrating-forehead up and down enthusiastically, with an encouraging look in my eyes.

'Influence is about shaping the opinions of other people. If you can do that, you can do anything. Be anything. And live for a long, long time. Oh, yes you can.'

She was nodding again, this time with her eyes fixed on the blue flames of the wall-mounted gas fire. Then she did something else she rarely did when we were alone: she drew a wide, pink smile across her dark face.

'You see, the only things of value in God's universe are other people's memories. By being careful, you can influence these memories so that you find a suitable place in there for yourself—one in which you appear exactly how you want. The truth of the matter is that my time, I mean our time… well, everyone's time I suppose, is limited. But what is also true is that the dead live on in the memories of the people they have touched. So, if you are careful, you can live on for hundreds of years. Just like Mother Theresa will. Are you following me? Are you?'

I nodded again, and she continued.

'When she dies, that nun will live on in the memories of all those people she helped. In fact, she will live even longer in the memories of their children and their children's children, because that is the kind of impact the woman has. Do you follow? She has been very careful. What a clever woman she is. And I am being careful too, child. And so should you.'

As for my father, Lily refused to entertain the subject.

'You don't have one. You never have, and you never will.'

The one time I challenged her on the biological impracticalities of her claim, she answered with a broom handle and screams of disgust. I still have the scar above my right eye from the stitches. I told the nurse that I'd hit myself while twirling the broom handle like a majorette's baton. But Lily threw the fiction back in my face and scolded me for lying to the nurse, and proceeded to tell her the truth. For weeks I lived in fear of social services knocking on our front door.

Aunt Liza was staying with us the day Lily announced that I had been an accident. I was lying on the rug in front of the mahogany veneered wall-mounted gas fire, my favoured part of the front room. Heat on my left, coffee table to the right, the shelf underneath where I'd keep my magazines, and the TV in front of me. Liza and Lily were on the sofa beyond the coffee table, and for most of the evening they may as well have been a world away—their words hummed and murmured outside my warm little den. Then, in a very matter-of-fact way, with a sentence that pierced my comfortable cocoon, she explained that I was a significant inconvenience and she would have preferred to have dedicated more of her life to her work instead of looking after that little mishap. She tutted as I ran out of the living room, crying.

'See what I mean?'

Her sharp words followed me through the door and up the stairs.

Later, Liza, dressed in her full-length nightgown, came into my room, sat on the edge of my bed, stroked my head and offered an explanation. Lily, she told me, was the youngest of seven: George Junior, Jerome, Little Annie, Agatha, Charles and Liza. Until then, I'd been under the impression that Liza was Lily's only sibling. My aunt made light of this and went on to tell me about my mother's first memory. It was of her eldest sister, Little Annie, who was fifteen at the time, pushing her to the ground and accusing her of killing their mother.

'Momma died as she gave birth to Lily, you see. So Papa was left in charge. But he couldn't manage with so many of us. So he asked his sister, your great-auntie Cecilia, to move in and help.'

Liza was the kind of person who forgets to look away from the listener when speaking at length. Her large, wet, brown eyes forced me to smile and nod as I listened.

'Papa was a loving man. You would have liked him. Yes, he had some shortcomings around the house, I suppose, but he knew how to keep us in line and make us feel like family. And he had a lot of time for Lily—she was the youngest, see. But then he went and died too. It was three years after momma's death, to the day. They said he was drinking a lot that night, and he slipped on the steps of the pub, hit his head. It was so terrible. All of us cried for days. God knows what it sounded like to the neighbours—seven children bawling their little hearts out for hours and hours.

'And then everything changed. With Papa gone there was a new pecking order, and your Momma found herself right at the bottom. Those following years were hell for her. Auntie couldn't control us, and the others were so mean to Lily. They blamed her, you see. They said she killed our Momma and, therefore, she killed Papa too. So they stopped speaking to her. They behaved like she wasn't there, which was worse. From the age of three, the poor thing didn't have a seat at the table, a bed to sleep on, or clothes to wear. They didn't make food for her, and they did everything they could to make sure she didn't get any kind of affection. I had to love her in secret. I used to sneak her food and let her into my bed while the others slept. But when they were around I had to pretend that she didn't exist.'

Liza's eyes now poured with tears and, although she was looking at me, I wasn't the person she saw.

'One by one, they left home until only Lily, me and Auntie were in the house. Things got better for a while but then I had to move out when I got married. I thought Lily would be okay, but Auntie wasn't good to her. I felt so guilty when I found out that Auntie had thrown her out when she found out she was pregnant with you. And...'

Her eyes left mine for the first time. It was just a flicker, a glance at the floor, and then they returned.

'I believe that if you are going to tell the truth you should tell all of it. So I'm sorry if it hurts to hear this. She wanted an abortion. It was difficult to arrange that kind of thing in those days, around here anyway, but it was possible and she could have managed it. But then your father said that, if she kept you, he would support her. So she agreed.'

'My father? You mean he basically saved my life?'

'I suppose so. But it was Lily's decision in the end.'

'Yeah, I know. But if he hadn't given her that option then I wouldn't be here, would I?'

'It's probably not a good idea to think too much on that.'

'And what about my dad? Who is he?'

'I don't know. I never met him. All you need to know is that he didn't keep his end of the bargain.'

'She must have told you.'

'She never has. I doubt she ever will.'

Liza asked me to promise I'd never mention this story to Lily, or anyone else, kissed me on the forehead and told me that she loved me.

———

Lily never spoke to me about her family, even though she spent so many years taking her revenge on them. Without Liza, I would never have seen what was happening. But even she didn't seem to understand what her sister was doing, despite being an accomplice. I watched as, one after another, Lily found chinks in their armour through which to drive her sword of kindness and compassion.

While they continued to ignore her during adulthood, Lily studied her brothers and sisters ardently. Through Liza's regular and highly detailed updates, Lily collated her intelligence. Liza visited most of her siblings regularly. Whenever it came to Lily's turn, she brought a little something from the cake shop and the two of them would talk for hours. Lily would listen intently to every word of her sister's reports, and over the years she compiled a list of personal tragedies to exploit. And one by one she worked on them, using her talents to make sure they had no choice but to pay her their fullest attention.

It began with Jerome's eldest son, Joshua. When he was a young teenager, the police were regular visitors to the house and it had been obvious for a while to Lily that the boy was Jerome's weakness. She struck when, aged seventeen, he was arrested for drug dealing. Using her church connections, she saved him from a prison sentence by enrolling him on an over-subscribed and under-funded rehabilitation programme for ex-gang members, a scheme the authorities looked favourably upon—and all charges were dropped.

Then it was Agatha's turn. This was a woman who resisted all companionship and attachments, and only tolerated Liza's monthly visit, often failing to be at home when she called. For many years the reconnaissance mission failed to turn up anything of interest. Then Lily got lucky—Agatha was diagnosed with cancer. She sent a card. Then some flowers. She left food parcels at her door. Then she called her up with offers of help and prayers. Every effort was met with the resistance of a dam. But she chipped away at her sister, taking note of the cracks when they appeared, until, eventually, Agatha caved in and accepted her help—and Lily had her where she wanted her.

Next up was the unemployable Charles. After too many dismissals to count, he was fired from the family home. Lily found him in hospital—he'd been attacked while sleeping rough in a park—brought him to her home and sent me to stay at Auntie Liza's. Having discovered his passion for cooking (enthusiasm, rather than flair), she set some ground rules and lent him the money to buy into a pizza shop franchise. The business worked and, in time, he moved back in with his family. Three years on, he repaid Lily and bought a second franchise.

At first, George Junior seemed to prefer being blackmailed to the verge of bankruptcy than accepting help from his sister. Then, one night he arrived with Liza at Lily's front door. There were tears and hugs, and he asked for forgiveness and help. He came clean about his extortioner—he'd ended a long-term affair with a woman who was now determined to take what she believed was rightfully hers. Calls were made and two elderly ladies from the church arrived at the house. They were given a cheque and instructions, and George Junior was told to go home. He never heard from the woman again.

And then, finally, there was Little Annie. Her weakness was a little more complex. Her husband was a successful businessman and was faithful to her. Her children were sensible, intelligent people who later became our family's first university graduates. She had friends and a healthy social life and, as there was no need, she chose not to work. On the surface, she was a fortress. But there is always a way in, and with

Little Annie it was remorse. The more she learnt about Lily and what she had done for their other siblings, the greater her shame grew. Over the course of several years, she appealed to Liza to arrange a meeting with Lily. But every time the request was delivered, Lily refused. When, at last, she was the only sibling not to be reconciled, the attempts grew more desperate and offers of money were made, as she declared she would not be left out in the cold. However, Lily decided that it would be in everybody's best interest if that were where she stayed.

———

I would wait until she fell asleep before I crept into her room. As slowly and as carefully as I could, I'd lie beside her, my face just centimetres from hers, and imagine I was a baby again. I would shrink to the size of a speck of dust and float next to her mouth and her nostrils, swaying in her breath. I would hover up to her eyelids and land on her lashes, where I'd stay until a gentle gust of air lifted me up so I could resume my tour of her face. Memories would appear from nowhere and mingle with my dreams and she would carry me in her arms, across a desert, through a deep forest, under the sea. We could see in the dark, breathe underwater, and float away from danger. And I was perfectly safe. Everything I needed was contained in that inch of warm air between us. The smell of her cleanser mixed with the lavender-scented pillow, and soon I was overcome and asleep next to my mother—almost in her arms.

————

'You will never get back.'

She said it quietly as she pulled me stiffly into her duffel-coated chest at the bus station. Physical affection from a rusty tractor. I was seventeen and on my way to a new job and a flat in London. Freedom was a coach ride away and I was like a cat ready to pounce.

'What you on about? 'Course I will. I'll be back next month for your birthday. I already told you that.'

'No, that is not what I mean, child.'

I pulled away from her and stared into her face. I hadn't been this close to her for years; it was uncomfortable.

'What, then?'

'When you are born your soul is given a special place in your community. When you take your soul away from where you belong, you leave that place forever. Another soul takes your space. Yes, you will come back. You might even decide to come back to live. You will come back, but you will never get back in. It'll never be the same for you here.'

————

I didn't make it back for her birthday. Perhaps because of her warning. Perhaps it was the distance or how busy I was. Later, it could have been her refusal to come to my new home, to meet my partner Alfie and newborn. As time passed, the bond fragmented and the need to see her dissolved. I sent a card, as I did for two decades. There were the telephone calls—awkward and infrequent—and it was during one of these when she informed me she was ill. And so I returned to her house nearly twenty years after I had left it.

Gone were the coffee table and antique-look television cabinet that never closed. The heavily patterned carpet, rich with swirling browns, yellows and dark reds, was now plain and light, mint green, and peppered with tiny tumbleweeds of newness. The fireplace was now a bookshelf that housed a large number of well-thumbed religious texts. The prints of English cathedrals that had once crammed the flock walls had disappeared and all that hung from the thick, off-white matt was an empty wooden crucifix, positioned over a rigid high-backed sofa. The wall that used to separate the living room and the dining room had also gone, and in its place was a large four-panelled door that opened like a giant glass concertina. Everything seemed ultra new and dust resistant, but phantoms remained. She still moved through the room so as not to collide with the coffee table, and when she came in from the cold she would warm the backs of her American-tan legs by the bookshelf as if the acidic blue flames were still there, hissing at her skirt.

She faced her cancer with the strength I expected. Everything was in order and there was no fear. She tutted at her physical weakness and pondered aloud about flushing her tablets down the toilet. Liza was now a permanent feature. She fluttered about her and occasionally found the courage to tell her not to be so silly. Agatha appeared daily. Unsure of her role, she spent her time there on the sofa, drinking tea and staring at the corner where the television used to be, rising like an accordion whenever help was needed.

———

We didn't find ourselves alone until three weeks after my return. Lily stood by the kitchen sink—her back to me. Her shoulders were high and her movements hesitant. She knocked the same empty tumbler over three times during our silence. Neither of us knew what was owed, but there were dues to be paid. I sat at the breakfast table and breathed deeply and quietly, and prepared for the reconciliation—imagining her corroded arms around me while a single tear dispersed on the tributaries of her face.

Still with her back to me:

'I have put an envelope in my bedside table drawer. It has everything you need in it.'

'Oh, okay.'

'My will is there, too. I am leaving some money to your son.'

'Thomas.'

'Yes.'

She pulled the plug from the sink and hobbled to the radiator and the towel.

'I'll get that.'

I rose like Agatha.

'Stay where you are!'

I felt every step that she took and saw for the first time that she was dying before my eyes. Cell by cell, shuffling towards the final assault.

'Everything else is going to the church.'

'Oh.'

'Do you need money? There is still time to change it.'

'No. I'm fine. Thanks.'

Hands dried, she replaced the towel and moved towards the open door.

'Right. I am going to bed.'

———

The house overflowed with black suits and darker moods. Despite mourners crowding into the front door and out of the back, the number was disappointing. The timing had not worked in Lily's favour. The Right Reverend Clement Hook had passed away on the same day, rendering her venue, master of ceremonies and two-thirds of her target audience, who thought it spiritually prudent to attend the bishop's funeral, unavailable.

I followed the pallbearers into the church and felt the sadness that hung in the air like a suspended tsunami. At the crematorium, I watched her coffin being placed onto the ceremonial conveyor belt and listened to the gasps of grief as the mechanical curtains severed our last moments with our community warrior. I led the mourners into the wake at the local Liberal club, and kept my distance from Lily's surviving sisters and brothers as they embraced her nephews and nieces, opened their hands to the heavens, and cried on demand. This was the epicentre of grief. Little Annie was there, shedding tears like a bereaved mother. The women in plastic garden chairs, the men surrounding them—one kneeling, with his head on the shoulder of a sister, the other two standing, resting their hands upon the tropical furniture. They acted as one. The moment one of them cried, the arms of this six-person creature stretched to the distressed part of its body and soothed itself with pats, rubs and mutterings.

The gentle chattering of the recently bereaved, the clinking of cups and saucers, and the clunking of pint glasses against wooden tables sheltered and calmed me. A little laughter eventually eased its way into the ambience and soon the audio became smooth, comforting waves of solace, as raw emotions blended with agreeable company. And I bathed in the clarity that remains when tears have washed away the pain.

Everyone around me turned and faced the source of the sound. One of my ancient aunts was refusing help to get out of her chair. It wasn't that her voice was particularly loud, just that those around her had fallen silent. Young women nudged their partners towards Little Annie, whose bony hands looked ready to crumble like chalk beneath her own weight as she pushed her frail body upwards. She barked at their approaches like a cornered dog.

'Do I look like a cripple?'

Her eyes spat at them. Nobody answered, preferring to revert to collective telekinesis to help her to her feet. She shuffled with excruciating slowness away from the family, and each time she lifted a foot, we held our breath until it landed safely. After she'd traversed ten metres or so, our confidence grew and the paranormal support relaxed. She crumpled to the ground, momentarily leaving her walking stick standing over her like a growling king cobra. From nowhere, a large space suddenly appeared around her, only to close in again more quickly. From the centre out, to a radius of about five or six people thick, bodies hunched towards the old woman on the floor. Beyond that a second, wider, layer appeared—one of people within earshot of the initial screams of surprise, each one of them facing the middle of the gathering, raising themselves on tiptoes to see what had happened. Soon, every person in the venue was trying to catch a glimpse of Little Annie.

————

'Thomas has been asking about you. He took ages to go down. He really misses you when you're not here.'

Alfie took my hand, kissed me and rested his forehead against mine.

'I don't miss you at all, though.'

He smiled, and I wrapped my arms around him and soaked up his warmth. I felt my shoulders fall and my bones soften.

'How was it?'

————

I have a childhood memory of painting outside. The weather was good and Lily had set me up in the garden with everything I needed, including a large jar of water that towered over everything else on the table. The jar cast a wide shadow and bright lines of white light danced across the paper and paints, and I traced their movements with my fingers. Then, with bristles loaded with thick yellow paint, I pushed my nose against the cold glass and dipped the paintbrush into it. Gas-like trails of colour felt their way into the cold water, lowering themselves down slowly, taking unexpected routes and finding invisible obstacles that caused them to suddenly blossom. Then, slowly, when all was calm, I pulled the brush out, charged it with a slightly darker colour, and repeated the process. I did the same again, each time with a deeper, contrasting paint, until the water was thick with pigment and the beauty was lost.

TAP TAP

Tap tap. Up the steps from the stone-floored cellar, through the thick oak door and into the vacant hallway and empty house.

Tap tap. Rattling the old brass bolt.

Tap tap. Once again. And once more again. Laconic and futile. Like ants climbing a lit match.

Silence and preservation. These were the themes of the project. His old breath sealed and concealed within careful mahogany boxes. Dovetails and wax. Seventy-two copper nails in each box, all hidden beneath his craftsmanship. His name and the date of discharge carved upon the lid. Tiny, French-polished halitosis coffins, big enough for a lungful. Exhale and shut. Carbon dioxide of his own making—his very own waste gases captured forever. And if one day they are unearthed from their burial pit, and if they are opened, he will breathe upon the future.

The method took time to master. This was not a man who knew how to make. This was an office man. A desk man. A man of letters and numbers. A man who did money—other people's gravy—and came home to a meal on the table, the news and a wife. Respected colleagues, a well-thought-of job, and a faltering interest in golf. Soft hands and smooth fingernails. A slight ache in his right forearm which he eased by alternating his mouse finger. Emails and spreadsheets. Conference calls and a company car. Figures, those he could manipulate. Forecasts he could craft. Wood, however, was alien and hostile. It took time to tame.

It brought peace. An unexpected benefit. A side effect of his 'hobby'. He never called it that. That was a word from others, like his wife. Uttered at dinner parties and during phone calls. He had a hobby, and that was good for a man of his years. He needed an interest. Healthy and wholesome. Every man should have one. Especially when so close to retirement. The faint and rhythmic sounds of sawing from behind the bolted door; the reassurance of hammer against nails. She was comforted because he had found something to keep him occupied while she flicked between televised makeovers.

There was a room in the office building. In the centre

of the open-plan area, feet away from his desk. For meetings and brainstorms. Glass walls and Venetian blinds. Its position, chosen to elevate the importance of these corporate activities, acted as a deterrent. But he would use it. Not enough to raise suspicion. Just once in a while. He would turn off the air conditioning unit and breathe. One hour was enough to suffuse the space if he filled his lungs to capacity. Slowly, so as not to hyperventilate, head in hands over random papers at the smoked glass table. His molecules mixing with the clean air, colliding with the incumbents until they reached every corner. Conquering the atmosphere. Out here his breath mingled with that of almost two hundred other people—a vile cocktail of human waste which he inhaled as shallowly as he could. But in there was pure him. Once, aroused by the thought of his gas penetrating the lungs of another, he left his papers on the table in the glass meeting room. He asked a junior worker, a young woman with dark hair and sculpted calves to fetch them. He watched her enter the chamber and walk to the papers. He counted the breaths she took—taking him inside her. Thirteen inhalations. A baker's dozen. Slipping into her smooth young throat and pink lungs.

His wife was confused when he stopped going to work. How could he be stressed? His life was blessed. He had a nice home, money was plentiful, the children were doing well. Pleasant friends and an active social life. He had her. She who had sacrificed so much to make life good for him. He didn't have to lift a finger. She could have been angry. She had every right. But she chose to support him. She always had. It was expected. Stress is an illness and she would cure him. Get him back to work. Even if it meant missing her favourite programmes from time to time. There were always the repeats.

Tap tap.

The boxes he buried in the meadow. That's what she called it. Land they left to rot at the bottom of the garden. It's good for the environment and all that, she said. She'd seen it on TV. Give nature some space to breathe the presenter had said. The trench was out of sight of the house. Behind the tall nettles and a growing mound of grass cuttings and uprooted weeds. He dug while she slept. Pushing the spade into the earth slowly and quietly. Then, when the caskets were covered, he'd sit and imagine the stillness inside. Small universes of tranquillity. Each one a cosmos of his making.

She watched from the dark bedroom, several feet away from the window so the moonlight would not reach her moisturised face. People bury victims in their gardens. She'd seen them on television. Elderly parents, prostitutes, stepdaughters and wives. She should be alarmed—that she knew. So she watched every night, his diaphanous silhouette bending over the inky hole. And through the day she turned down the volume and listened to him behind the bolted cellar door. As long as she knew where he was everything would be fine.

The project grew. Its ambition ballooned, as did the time it demanded. Emerging from the brick-clad warren only to eat and to defecate, he toiled through the days, spurred on by a need to dig deeper into the stillness. Imagination was failing him. He needed the reality of the box. To feel the blackness around his body. Thick, ancient wood to protect him. Its gentle hardness severing time. Cutting the empty umbilical cord. A freedom and beauty of nothingness were waiting for him.

This was a pragmatic man. A reasonable man. A man who knew that to dive into the stillness in all its purity required permanence. There would be no way out of the box. Purity requires conclusiveness. And finality requires death. But a thread still ran from him to his job, current affairs, to his wife and children. And while that fibre had thinned and weakened until there was only shadow, enough remained to tug at his proprieties. His escape from the box was a necessity. Though it could not be of his own doing. A self-initiated release soiled the clarity of his pursuit. The escape would enter the silence with him. It would speak to him. When? Now? The noise would be unbearable. This was a man who knew he could not extinguish such a thought. He needed an accomplice —someone unsuspecting and totally reliable.

She used to look forward to mealtimes. His starter on the table as he walked through the front door. They would kiss and he would watch the news on the portable while she finished cooking the main course. As they ate he would tell her about the world and compliment her culinary endeavours. Now he ate alone. She waited on the other side of the dining room door until the metal stopped scraping the ceramic. Until the cellar door closed again. Until the tapping resumed. Then she would eat. Conversation was a thing of the past. The occasional hello. A nod. So she was surprised to hear him speak to her. The meal lay steaming on the table behind him. His voice sounded different. Older, perhaps. He had worn the same clothes for days. The suits, the groomed hair. The clean-shaven face. The pride in his appearance that had, on occasion, embarrassed her. All that belonged to another man. There was a stranger in her house. A man whose voice she didn't recognise. In his right hand he held a yellow crowbar.

'Do you know what this is?"

This is why she should have acted sooner. This is why she should have called someone about the hole in the garden. This is the moment the TV news reporters would describe after her body had been found. If it was ever found.

She nodded and backed slowly into the dining room.

'Will you come downstairs tonight?'

He may have said this but she couldn't be sure. It was as if he wasn't speaking English. His words fell over one another, like drunks out of the pub.

'Tonight. At nine o'clock. Will you come down to the cellar?'

The diction was precise this time. He had cleared his throat, enunciated slowly, and lowered the weapon.

She swallowed and the predicament fell to the pit of her stomach. He muttered something about it being important. He needed her. Something to do with his work. She was the only person he could count on. All she could do was agree. Nod her head and hope that this was enough.

Tap tap.

It was a masterpiece. Outer dimensions measured six foot by three. A two-inch wall of oak, lined with one-inch wide strips of mahogany and rosewood. He sat on the first stone step and stared at his creation. A man like him had made a thing like this. It was beautiful. Inside and out, the attention to detail was outstanding. There were parts he could barely remember working on. The hand-carved border where the side panel would meet the heavy lid; the precise dovetail joints of contrasting grains; the thick, seamless brass edging that appeared to carry the entire casket, as if holding it above the cold hard floor. The lid was attached along the far width by three large brass hinges. From its inside lip protruded forty-four iron spikes that he had sharpened until he dared not touch their points. Each one carefully angled and positioned to ensure maximum penetration into the wood below. All he had to do was knock away the broom handle and the lid would fall and seal him inside.

At 6pm he placed his knife and fork into the centre of his plate and thanked his wife for his meal. She looked more nervous than usual, but then so did he. It was a big night. She had an important role to play, and he could tell by the way she stood at the sink and watched him eat that she understood. There was no need to say anything. He rose and walked to the cellar door, leaving the crowbar on the table.

She noticed that he did not slide the bolt. She heard his footsteps echo against the bare brick as he descended the stairs. When they stopped, she opened the cloakroom door, reached for the suitcase and placed it on the floor. Then she took her coat, hung it neatly over her arm, picked up her shoes by the straps and tiptoed to the front door, the weight of the case causing the floorboards to creak beneath her feet.

She had planned to leave the front door ajar to cut down on unnecessary noise, but once outside she ceased to care and she pulled it hard. The sound masked the thud from the cellar as the heavy lid landed perfectly in place.

It was far more beautiful than he had imagined. The thick, warm air embraced him, and the darkness— deeper than he ever thought possible—drew his senses from his body and extended them far into the nothingness. Soon he was speeding through millennia, spanning time that had yet to exist. He was no longer a self-contained creature, but a cloud of atoms scattering in all directions, bursting through dimensions; tearing down the fabric of the cosmos—he was everywhere, every moment and everything. And out of the dark, impossible colours engulfed his infinite journeys, tracing each trajectory and revealing the knowledge of the universe. He saw the paradox of emptiness; the energy of nothing; the enormity of fathomless expansion. He swam through a blackness so deafening it was as if Creation itself was speaking to him—an excited and dangerous child, unburdening itself of the secrets it had hidden for eternity. Truths the size of universes showed themselves, one after another, strobing into his brain, pounding him, demanding his acceptance. And universes the size of dust particles filled his mouth and nostrils—blankets of hot stars from every corner of totality stuffed themselves deep into his lungs. From the furthest point, a fleck hurtled towards him. At first he took it for another colossal revelation preparing to explode into his consciousness. He was unperturbed by its speed and the harshness of its light. But as it grew closer he recognised it as something different. This was to be the big reveal. This was to change everything—the final secret that would unlock it all. As he braced himself for impact, he became aware of his body for the first time and, in doing so, his environment reasserted itself. He remembered that he was waiting for something. The hardness below him pressed into his hip and shoulder, and the final revelation arrived. Not in his head like the others, but in his chest. So hard that he could not breathe. Everything had come to him in these dark moments—everything except her. There was nothing left in here now. Nothing to see and nothing to breathe. He reached out, clenched his fist and tapped his knuckles on the wall of the box.

ROCCO FELLINI'S FAMOUS MASHED POTATOES

If in possession of a good ear and an appreciation for the auditory delights of fine dining, and if positioned correctly—equidistant from the grand oak and glass entrance and the large, perpetually swinging double doors that led to the kitchen—it was quite possible to perceive two distinct acoustic fabrics. The first floated so high above the diners that it caressed the painted ceiling.[1] This layer of sound was a delicate web of cut glass spun from the minute clinks and tinkles of heavily laden decanters that flirted with the rims of crystal goblets. The other quite different: a tightly woven, silver-porcelain blanket knitted from the sound of two hundred pairs of knives and forks striking the bone china with such frequency that, to the human ear, it seemed constant and singular. While no more than a membrane, this second veneer was somewhat heavier than its acoustic sister and wafted its familiar and reassuring waves against the necks of the restaurant's guests.

If capable of enjoying such a sonic banquet, it was also entirely possible to detect one notable absence. Typically and traditionally, in the exceptional restaurants of Castleport, a third skin of sound would be present. This layer always emanated from the kitchens. The distant and often muffled ensemble of meat cleavers against wood and bone, sharpening stone against steel, whisking and hushed beratings, frying and bubbling, searing and chopping, oven doors closing and rushed footsteps combined to create a subtle cadence—a full percussive spectrum that blended to each establishment's particular timbre. Most notable were L'Agonie on Albert's Lane, and Stonato off Finch Square. The former was home to the frequent screams of anguish of a much-loved sous with high but impractical standards. Diners at the Italian restaurant, on the other hand, were treated to morsels of operatic choruses performed by the amateur voices of the entire kitchen every time a waiter opened the doors. The kitchen here, however, was silent.[2] The omission was significant as this restaurant belonged to a man known for his insistence on silence in the work environment: Rocco Fellini, the invisible[3] chef.

However, for the most part, common diners were less well attuned to the auditory delights of fine dining, and the aforementioned beautifully crafted acoustic layers were, to them, indiscernible behind the thick slick of fat, wealthy voices that coated chairs, tables and windows, fouled the deep, luxurious carpet, and bloated its way along the densely decorated walls.

It was from that quagmire, on this particular evening, a large shape began to emerge from somewhere near the central tables. The gourmand's giant shoulders strained as they pushed through the first layer of sound. Once this had been achieved, the rich ooze melted from him, and the top of his naked crown touched the sonic web, which caused him to scratch his damp, bald head as he waded his way towards the kitchen.

Inside, the kitchen-hands began to tremble as soon as their master halted his activities. Of late, they had sensed unease in Fellini; his handling of food had been less loving, and his treatment of his employees less caring. They had witnessed a steady but devastating deterioration in his magical creativity. The man they loved, the reason why they tolerated the unreasonable hours, the unendurable heat and the impossible pay, was suffering. They mourned their loss, and whispered of debts, bad blood and ill health. And now, at this unprecedented cessation of cooking, during the first sitting of all things, they realised that whatever their unseen master had been dreading was well on its way.

'WHERE'SFELLINI?' boomed the gourmand, as the door separating the kitchen and the dining room burst open, shattering the elbow of a young kitchen-hand.

'WHERETHEFUCKISFELLINI?'

The other kitchen-hands grabbed their wounded colleague and scuttled under stoves, into unused ovens and behind drawers, cupboards and sinks; anywhere that would shield them from the double-breasted beast that had just smashed their silent order to smithereens of smithereens. Each time he opened his mouth to enquire after the famous chef more hands disappeared until, from where the monster stood, the kitchen was empty.

With nobody left to bellow at, the gourmand rested his gargantuan rear against a cupboard unit, his immense weight slamming it back against the wall, crushing to death three hands who had been hiding behind it.

In the middle of the kitchen stood a large, irregularly shaped table that held twenty-eight enormous plates of exotic fruits, stuffed reptiles, multi-coloured meats, exquisite desserts and so much more than the human eye could possibly hope to digest in one sitting. The gourmand had never before seen so many dishes he did not recognise assembled in one place. Greens, yellows, blues even, danced around the table mesmerising him. Fist-sized globules of white food-stuff floated up from the table and organised themselves into neat half-spheres. Through his overfed eyes, the gourmand saw that the floating food was being arranged onto a reflective circular dish from which sharp spears of light were slashing their way towards him. Before he could act, the blinding shards lanced his retinas, causing him to become unsteady on his feet and to grab a nearby oven, disturbing another ineffectual hiding place.

'I'm sorry, sir, but you're going to have to leave.' The deep monotone belonged to none other than Pico Olive, the maître d', who, in the ruckus, had somehow managed to position himself directly in front of the gourmand.

'This is no place for you, sir. Please…' Olive gestured towards the door the large bald man had crashed through.

'…if you would be so kind.'

'I'MHERETOSEEFELLINI', the gourmand turned his prodigious head towards the Olive's, 'ANDI'MNOT-GOINGANYWHEREUNTILIHAVE.'

The hairs on head waiter's head fluttered in the roar.

'I believe you know that is not possible, sir.'

The gourmand breathed in slowly and deeply, dragging every droplet of scent in through his wide, moist nostrils. As he opened his mouth in preparation to exhale, the gentle clunk of glass against wood caused him to halt and turn back to the table, where the reflective dish was now resting. The circular arrangement of mashed potato[4] was now at least one foot deep.

'Come, sir. The other guests are waiting to be served.' The maître d's voice was now notably higher pitched, 'I'm afraid you're in danger of spoiling their evening.'

But the gourmand remained where he was, sprawled across the cupboard and the oven, and smiled at the large plate of mashed potato.

'IMAYNOTBEABLETOSEEHIM.'

He paused.

'BUTICANTOUCHHIM.'

And with that, he rolled towards the table. Butchers blocks, kitchen carts and worktops dived out of his path. Exposed kitchen-hands ran for their lives, sometimes successfully. The gourmand's progress was cumbersome but swift, and in very little time he had ploughed his way to the large plate where, suddenly, he faltered. Although he sensed that Fellini was standing right there beside him, the intruder was now welded to the spot on which he stood. For there on the table in front of him, like the sacrificial lamb, lay the master's work—Fellini's famous mashed potatoes. Now, what mortal could resist such a temptation? The salivary glands that do not bubble when presented with a feast like this belong to the tongue of a dead man, and even then there may be a little spray. A rare wind of doubt blew through the gourmand's fat head. Was the presence he felt emanating from the invisible chef himself, or merely from his creation? As he pondered, the surviving kitchen-hands fought amongst themselves to surround the invader as fast as they could; fifteen sinewy assistants swarmed around the giant's legs. Pushing and shoving ensued as they tried to manoeuvre him away from where the food lay, and from where they suspected their master to be. Underestimating the physical persuasion they could exert on a man of such magnitude, the kitchen-hands thrust with more force than the gourmand could resist and he began to lose balance. Turning from pondering, the gourmand leant against the direction of his impending fall but, as his legs tangled in the bodies of several kitchen-hands, equilibrium eluded him and he fell chest-first into the mound of mashed potato.

The maître d' had the hands drag the unconscious, heavy body outside through the back of the restaurant, along with the corpses of their colleagues and destroyed kitchen furniture. On their return from the cold alleyway, they were surprised to see their beloved headwaiter kneeling, tears flowing from his eyes. As they approached, what had happened became apparent. On the floor in front of Pico Olive, among the smashed fodder, in the centre of the gourmand's chest imprint, they could depict a significantly smaller impression. And the kitchen hands knew that Olive was weeping over the crushed body of Rocco Fellini.

In the dining room, all of the guests, including those lacking the ability to appreciate the auditory delights of fine dining, were aware of a change in ambience. Despite it, they continued to enjoy the food and drink that had been placed before them as best they could, preferring not to speak of the noises from the kitchen. Soon, however, as it became apparent that the empty decanters were unlikely to be refilled and their plates would not be replenished, and as the subtle acoustic layers evaporated, they began to leave. Some left money on the tables and moved awkwardly to the exit, casting furtive glances towards the kitchen doors, hopeful that they would suddenly burst open as a troop of waiters laden with dishes and wine re-entered the room; while others vacated in anger, knocking over empty chairs and glasses as they did so. Later, when they heard the news, the guests would quietly regret their impatience and would wish they had remained seated. Perhaps they would have caught a glimpse of the masters' slight outline as his body was removed from the restaurant on a stretcher, under a white silk sheet. Maybe they would have been invited to join the staff as they feasted on that final batch of Rocco Fellini's now legendary famous mashed potatoes.

---

1. In 1902, a respected Chinese muralist fell upon hard times. Stranded in Castleport after a disastrous commission for the wife of a cousin of King Edward VII, the artist made a proposal to Rocco Fellini, a young Italian chef and the owner of a new restaurant in town. In exchange for food and board for one year, the artist would create a mural to rival the beauty of the Sistine Chapel on the ceiling of the restaurant. The chef agreed and the work began immediately. For twenty-three months, the muralist only rested while guests ate at the tables below, and the establishment soon became famous for the evolving artwork. Patrons spent as much time looking up as they did at their meals, and the restaurant critics of the day found that, after visiting, they wrote about the art as much as they did about the food and wine.

2. It was widely understood by his contemporaries that Fellini believed vibrations in the air had detrimental effects on several delicate procedures that took place in his kitchen. All kitchen staff were made to wear a specially commissioned design of slipper and were under strict orders not to speak while working.

3. Invisibility was, of course, a rarity, and for that the Sicilian was well known. His fame spread across Europe and beyond, and prestigious visitors from as far as Tokyo reserved their tables up to twelve months in advance, which, at that time, was unprecedented. However, despite numerous requests from the restaurant manager and Fellini's publicist, the chef refused to 'perform' for the benefit of diners and the novelty wore thin after four or five years of the restaurant opening.

4. His unfortunate lack of visibility and the associated celebrity aside, Fellini's pre-eminence in the upper echelons of culinary

mastery was due to his mashed potato. It first came to public note in the winter of 1904, when a prominent critic of the time, Anthony Sellbeck, wrote in The Times that *"The ambrosial white stuff transcends human articulation. Only in heaven might we find the words that may begin to describe this wonder"*.

ONCE A CIVIL SERVANT

Thinking was not one of my responsibilities at the Department but I didn't let that stop me. There were many favourable aspects of the job, and the opportunity to exercise my imagination was the best of them. Days would pass without me having to apply myself too rigorously to administrative issues, leaving me ample space in which to develop my theories. Now that the State no longer requires my services, and I have significantly more time available, I am writing a book about them. Commercially it will be challenging. They are a far cry from the uplifting, psycho-pop drivel found on the shelves of every train station bookshop across the country. But they are pragmatic. My book will be a practical guide to living. And, I suppose, dying.

Towards the end of my employment (I didn't know that it was drawing to a close, but I am told I should have expected it), I happened upon a concept that would change my life. It was, and is, a defining proposition that knits many of my other theories together so well and so tightly there is no doubt that it is the truth. I remember the epiphany well. Sitting at my desk in the open plan office in Whitehall, which had been my quiet sanctuary for 34 years to the day, I was so struck by my discovery that I stood up and knocked my chair to the floor. And as I stood there, staring back at the surprised faces that looked up from their computer monitors, I knew I had understood something so profound it would transform the way these people thought about the nature of their existence. Even now, as I escort my clients, such as poor Marsha here, away from their lives of misery, I am still spellbound by the significance of my hypothesis.

I call it The Three Deaths (it is likely that this will be the title of the book—I will, of course, invent a suitably provocative subtitle as is the trend). At its foundation is the notion that, contrary to popular belief, we will, as the title suggests, die three times. I used to think of it in terms of inevitable stages of death—a train that, once boarded, does not stop until it reaches its final destination. Then, as the idea developed, I realised that with intervention it is possible to halt the process before its conclusion. In other words, I know how to cheat death.

The first of these deaths I call Permanent Death. This

is the one we are expecting. The one in which the brain and heart stop functioning. The one that, as far as medical science is concerned, draws a definitive line under your story. The end, if you like.

My breakthrough was the realisation that this is not the end. Not quite. While, as the name suggests, there is no way back from Permanent Death, there is a postscript—a small addendum that is hidden from view until the final page is turned. Your irreversible departure is actually the beginning of an invisible finale that will last until True Death and Perceived Death have also been accomplished.

True Death occurs as the final trace of life leaves your body, which can happen a considerable time after the death certificate has been signed. The speed is dictated by the nature of your expiry. Natural causes, for instance, can take weeks. Poisoning also. No wounds, you see. Life requires an escape route. Violent episodes that result in holes on the body where there shouldn't be any, such as the one in poor Marsha's throat, are much faster.

Let us consider the case at hand. Life is still in the process of decamping from this woman's body. The bleeding has ebbed, but colour continues to spill like a geyser of thick, lazy paint. Bright yellows and reds and blues belch from the wound and swirl drunkenly into the air and splash onto the resin floor. It's like a volcanic rainbow. And until these colours have gone, there is still life in her body. Weak, unsalvageable life. The thing about True Death is that it never hurries—it takes its time to coil around a frame and squeeze every last drop of life from it.

Considerable skill is required to see the life as it escapes, and it has taken me many attempts to master it. It is a matter of letting your gaze drift as you might in a daydream. Your eyes are open but you look at nothing. Then, at the precise place in your field of vision where you least expect to see anything, there it is—as bold and as vivid as a freshly excavated, pumping heart. The initial release is often spectacular. One might compare it to a firework display. I haven't yet had the opportunity to watch a 'natural death', that is, sans escape hatch, but I imagine the show is rather disappointing in comparison.

That brings us to the third death, the speed of which is quite different. Perceived Death is remarkable in that it is not determined by how you die, but by how you live. You are not truly dead in this context until the people who knew you are made aware of your demise. Those who contributed to society—likeable characters who played constructive roles in their communities and families—are likely to have their passings noted quickly. Hours. Minutes, perhaps. It depends on individual circumstances. But those who hide while alive are also hidden in death. Knowledge of death is the thing. Without that, you will continue to exist in the lives of others. And even when there is plausible suspicion that death has occurred—if an individual disappears, for example—without proof, without official word even, there is still a chance that he or she is alive, and Perceived Death is thus suspended indefinitely.

If more people were aware of this final passage of death, the world would be a better place. I have no time for religious dogma. However, I do think that the majority of churches are on to something when they preach that doing the will of whichever deity one happens to follow is beneficial. It is interesting, don't you think, that these doctrines teach that living a good life is primarily in the interests of the individual, resulting in some kind of eternal reward, as if the benefits to the wider community are nothing more than a happy side effect. Where these institutions have it wrong is, instead of earning you a place in heaven or the happy hunting grounds or wherever, a 'good life' simply means that you are allowed to die quickly and fully. And what more can a person ask for? To slip gently into the stream and away—to be washed down to the black sea and back to where you came from. The alternative is to be snagged on a cold, wet rock until your loved ones acknowledge your expiry. There is a tendency to believe that grief is the property of mourners. That is also wrong. It does belong to them, yes, but they give it to the deceased. The oil of our tears smooths the souls of the dead past the rocks in the cold river and aids their delivery to the sea. That is what Perceived Death offers the deceased.

Poor Marsha has not had the benefit of this sorrowful lubricant, and right now she is marooned on her rock. If everything goes to plan, she will stay there for a long time to come.

I tell people that I work with the homeless. That's how it is these days—everyone wants to know what you do for a living. They ask you the second after you've revealed your name. They like to place you into a little box with a carefully inscribed label. It makes them comfortable and gives them the pointers they require to behave towards you in a manner they consider to be the most appropriate—whether deference or disrespect or, if they are feeling gracious, parity. So, I tell people I work with the homeless. That's usually enough. They usually fill in the gaps themselves. I'm probably some kind of social worker or something equally obnoxious. In the unlikely event of my answer attracting more questions, I turn the conversation onto them—which they lap up like neglected puppies.

The fact is I am a civil servant. It is irrelevant that I am no longer employed by the Department. I helped administer this country for over thirty years—doing my duty during good times and bad. You can't simply walk away from a life like that. Once a civil servant, forever a civil servant. When I cleared my desk at Whitehall, I took my sense of duty with me. I now run a small social enterprise that is currently funded by the European Union. Its mission to get homeless people off the streets. I help these pathetic creatures escape their miserable lives. And let me tell you, they are always grateful. Of course, they are. Who wouldn't be? I mean, would you like to live on these streets? In a state of permanent hunger, cold and fear? They have no hope, and I don't promise to fix that. I don't promise to improve their lives—I merely offer an escape.

Perhaps it would be beneficial to explain with the help of Marsha here. I don't know her real name, of course. It doesn't do to get to know the clients. Simplicity is everything in work like this. But it is useful to call them something.

Very early morning is the best time to look for new clients, when there are plenty of drunken fools staggering home. I pick the busiest streets—the ones nearest the clubs and late-night pubs—where I am just another invisible reveller. I always bring a freshly grilled burger or two, which I cook on the small electric stove at the workshop. I put them into sesame seed topped rolls and wrap them in kitchen foil to retain the heat.

I found Marsha in the doorway of a music shop on Joshua Street. She was hidden under a bundle of blankets and cardboard—set far back from the road, deep into the recessed entrance lined with windows full of electric guitars and saxophones and such likes, all behind a thick metal grill. I stopped, lit a cigarette and watched for a while. I find this practice helpful as it gives me the chance to see how the situation feels in my gut—there is no point wasting European taxpayers' money on someone who will refuse my help. Anyway, instinct told me this person would appreciate my efforts, so I sat down where I assumed her feet where. Her head burst from the blankets the second my rear touched the ground. When she eventually focused on me, her freckly, creased face looked unsurprised, and she sank back under her covers—only a tuft of red hair remained. Drugs were likely to blame for her lack of interest. They have a habit of taking the danger out of situations. I mean to say, I could have been anyone.

I waited a few minutes before speaking.

Much of this business is about empathy. Emotional intelligence was not a prerequisite to work for the Department. In fact, I'd venture to suggest it was a hindrance. We dealt with numbers, not people. I was often appalled at the ruthlessness of our tactics—how we could, with a quick signature, reduce a benefit payment and expose thousands of families to abject poverty—or design legislation that consigns disabled people to ritual humiliation of having to beg for welfare. Discussions about how—or where—people would live were frowned upon. We were little more than tools to aid the movement of the ideological pendulum swing. Empathy only got in the way.

'Aren't you going to say hello?'

It is important to hold a smile on one's face during these encounters—even if you think you are not being observed. I suspected she was watching me through a gap in the blankets.

'Are you still in there?'

There was a muffled grunt that sounded like she may have told me to go away in the Anglo-Saxon.

'Are you hungry?'

I threw a wrapped burger near to the tuft of hair. Dirty fingers emerged and pulled it under.

'In case you're wondering, I don't expect anything in return.'

At this point, it is prudent to let the client have some time to consume the food and assess the situation. Rushing often leads to unsatisfactory results. If patience is on my side, I sometimes wait until they speak to me. This is how it was with Marsha.

'Have you got any more food?'

Her question, her vaguely northern accent and the poorly hidden desperation in her intonation told me that she was indeed a perfect client.

'I do. But not here.'

She pushed her back up against the side of the doorway and opened a gap in the blankets. Pale skin, perhaps forty years old, probably quite handsome in her day, but hardship had taken its toll.

'The thing is, I work with people like you who are sleeping rough and help them find a way out. That's my job. I can give you more food. That's an easy thing to do. Or I can sort things for you so that you are never hungry or cold ever again. And I can guarantee that you'll never have to sleep in another doorway for the rest of your life.'

It took a little time for my words to process.

'I don't know.'

'That's okay. I'm not going to force you. If this is to work, you have to really want it. But I understand if you'd rather not. I realise that some people actually quite like their lives on the street.'

I leaned forward as if preparing to get up.

'No, wait. Can I think about it?'

'Of course. You have a little think. I am going to have a walk around the block and see if I can help somebody else. If I don't find anyone, I'll come back.'

'What if you do find someone else?'

'Well, I can only work with one client at a time. The

work is quite intense. So if I do find someone who wants help I have a duty to deal with them first.'

'Oh, right.'

'But, you know, if you're not ready yet I can come back in a month or two to see if you're still around.

'If I say yes, what happens next?'

'Well, we go to my office and make the necessary arrangements. But look, perhaps you're not ready for this. It's a service for homeless people who've had enough and want to end it. If you're not ready to end it, then we'd be wasting each other's time.'

It's not unusual for the conversation to run this way. Many people like this, particularly females and the young, are propositioned on a depressingly regular basis. There are a lot of unscrupulous characters around these days who think nothing of abusing them, often trading a dry bed and a hot meal for sexual favours. Quite frankly, it disgusts me. I hate to see people taking advantage of the burgeoning home-less population. While the country buckles under the weight of debt, these maggots think of nobody but themselves. As for me, it's all about the social impact. Every time I help a client escape, society benefits. The benefit to the client is obvious. The financial gain to the state is enormous—sometimes running into the hundreds of thousands of pounds. Consider the cost of police time, rehabilitation, housing, welfare and counselling, all of which make up an unwieldy process that might eventually result in the client being freed from homelessness and into gainful, tax-paying employment. More often than not, however, the system fails, the client ends up back on the streets and the costs start all over again. My system is failsafe and saves hardworking taxpayers millions.

What do I get from it personally? The answer to that is very little, but it is enough. I get satisfaction from knowing that my efforts are helping our country through these difficult times. While ineffectual politicians tinker around the edges with cuts to this or that service or benefit payment, I get down to the crux of the matter and make a real and lasting difference. So there is some pride in that.

Needless to say, Marsha quickly reconsidered and accepted my help. I told her how pleased I was and we walked to the workshop, talking a little about the weather on the way. I always take clients the long route just to make sure that they are feeling quite weary by the time we arrive.

I rent the workshop from the Local Authority. They are very accommodating to new social enterprises. Twelve months of discounted rent and no business rates to pay. The front office is arranged to look as if a few people work here. Four desks, two of them with computers (paid for by a grant from the EU). Coffee mugs and empty sandwich wrappers, and a few papers scattered around the place—it really seems to put clients at their ease. I call it a workshop as that's what it used to be. In many ways it still is, I suppose. I converted it myself with the help of numerous online videos. I have to admit I am rather impressed with my efforts. Before beginning this enterprise, I was a DIY virgin. However, having installed a floating ceiling complete with polystyrene tiles, plastered and painted the walls, and fitted a hardwearing carpet, very similar to the one at the Department, I now consider myself to be pretty handy. I even managed to work out a way of fixing a safe into the floor so that its door is flush with the boards. When the carpet is laid over it, there is no indication whatsoever of there being something underneath. The only thing slightly out of place is the small fridge in the corner of the room, but nobody has thought to ask about it yet.

I asked Marsha to take a seat at one of the desks and gave her a form to fill out. This, I think, is a stroke of genius. It's an A4 piece of white paper, headed with the words London Homeless Outreach in maroon. Underneath, it asks the client to complete their date of birth, last registered address, country of origin, and so on. There's even an optional ethnicity multiple choice for good measure. Any remaining doubts evaporate at this point.

While Marsha scribbled and ticked with a pencil, I put on my reading glasses and pretended to busy myself with something suitably administrative. Then, taking the form, I told her that I would make a few phone calls. I asked if she would like to rest while I did that. They always say yes. By this time, clients trust me and think nothing of the fact that the small, windowless chamber I direct them to contains a plastic coated couch and paper sheets, and has been designed for easy cleaning. The walls and floor are covered in a light green resin, and where you would expect to see a skirting board, there is a seamless, curved join. Opposite the bed there is a short hosepipe wrapped around a wall-mounted tap, below which there is a large plughole. The 'en suite' is accessed through a door at the far end of the room. I fitted all of it myself.

I keep it warm in there. Clients are often heavily dressed during winter, which can cause problems later. The heat encourages them to shed a few garments and loosen whatever remains. This, however, is the only comfort I give them. There is no food or drink, and conversation is kept to a minimum. I think it necessary to maintain a professional distance so they realise they are not home and dry just yet. The chamber has the feel of a hospital room for practical reasons, of course, but also to communicate that their stay is temporary and they will be moving on very soon.

Holding the handset to my ear, I pointed to the corridor where the room is located. Before giving

Marsha directions, I began my fake telephone conversation.

'Hi Jim, it's me. Just hold on a sec, will you? I have a new client with me.'

Then I looked at her over my glasses.

'Sorry. Second door on the right down there. I'll be about an hour, so make yourself at home in there. And feel free to lock the door.'

She disappeared down the corridor as I continued my conversation. It is essential to be able to do this for up to half an hour as the client may be listening. It isn't easy talking to an imaginary associate for any length of time, and I used to find it quite a challenge. Now, though, I have a mental script to run through, peppered with appropriated jargon and a measured amount joviality. The impression I am trying to give is that of two long-term co-workers going through a routine they have performed hundreds of times before. If the client is listening from the corridor, this lays another comfort blanket over any returning doubts.

When the door of the chamber is locked, it activates a red light over the entrance to the corridor (another triumph, if I may say so myself). This is the signal for me to change my clothes. In my drawer I keep a collection of disposable paper overalls, complete with hood and feet, and a box of latex gloves. It is usual at this stage for me to begin to feel the strain. It is a very stressful job, and this manifests itself in a racing heart and profuse sweat. So, rather than put the overalls on over my clothes, I strip first. The air circulates under the paper fabric and helps keep me comfortable. Then I lie on the floor with my body facing the ceiling and wait.

It's simply a case of remaining in this position until the moment feels right. I have become aware in recent weeks that there is an art to the timing. Its exact nature is difficult to characterise, and I have no way to describe it other than to say that I listen with my entire body until I sense a certain 'balance' has been reached. I know it sounds rather grandiose, but it's as if the universe tells me when the moment is right. The first time it happened I was lying on the floor in an attempt to calm my pulse. After several minutes, the air seemed to start vibrating as if a deep sound, too low for human ears to detect, was emanating from the cosmos—and I knew it was time.

This is how it was with Marsha.

I rose to my feet, pulled the carpet back to reveal the safe, opened it and retrieved an old honing rod, and selected a handmade Damascus blade from my collection. I ran the edge of the blade over the steel six times and put the rod back into the safe, closed it and replaced the carpet.

In the corridor, I unlocked the chamber door from the outside and entered.

I hypothesise that until all three deaths have occurred the subject cannot be considered dead. Yes, 'alive' would be a gross overstatement, but 'dead' is incorrect. Perhaps her status would be best described as 'suspended'. I won't pretend that I know what happens to a person when the cycle has not been completed (I have one or two theories, of course, but nothing I would hang my hat on just yet). However, I am confident that, for my clients, it is better than the misery experienced prior to my intervention. It is also worthwhile noting that my clients collude, albeit unintentionally, to halt the death process. They have excluded themselves from society and cut ties with their family and friends. I play no part in that. I like to think of it as their payment to me. My insurance policy, if you like. What do I mean by that? Think back, if you will, to the social nature of my enterprise. My work has a significant positive impact on the community. However, I am under no illusions, and I suspect that (due to a few fashionable cultural prejudices and, no doubt, a certain amount of wilful misunderstanding the complex nature of my work may evoke) wider society is simply not ready to accept my methods. That is why my clients' self-imposed exile is useful. As nobody will shed a tear of grief, death in the fullest sense has not occurred and, therefore, nothing unlawful has taken place.

As soon as I am satisfied there is no more life in the carcass, I will dispose of it in the usual way. The design of the chamber enables me to do all of the carving and bagging in an efficient manner. Once it is all done, I hose it all down and I am ready for my next client. The only flaw as far as I can see is the location of the refrigerator. I should probably move it into the chamber so I don't have run the risk of making a mess on the floor as I walk through the office with the meat I save for the burgers.

THE WIND ON JOSHUA STREET

Mary Little plunges her rubber-clad fist into the last toilet of the day. Soon she will remove her protective clothing, wash her hands, put on her coat, and walk out of the Leonard & Mann office block. Her route home will take her past the bus terminal where the first shift will just be arriving. Bleary-eyed and half asleep, the drivers will walk past her in the opposite direction, staring vaguely at their feet. She won't look at them and, if she's lucky, they'll do her the same courtesy. But Mary isn't lucky. Luck drifts past her and doesn't look up. Luck fails to notice her standing there as he serves pints of good fortune at the bar. Luck avoids eye contact because he's forgotten her name, and gives the breaks to the next person to circumnavigate any awkwardness. Luck is a bastard. The best she can hope for is causation. A cuddle and a kiss from Carlos in the kitchen if she gets home in time to prepare his breakfast before he leaves for work. If not, a peck on her cheek at the front door as they pass one another, or a wave from the upstairs bus window as he's driven past her. Whatever way, it's down to her, not luck. It was too late for luck now anyway. What good would he bring her out here? Find a ten-pound note on the pavement, get a smile from a good-looking driver, maybe bump into someone she knows? What would be the point? What can ten pounds buy you these days in this town? And what's the value of a smile or a surprise reunion when you smell of bleach and shit?

Then she'll climb up Joshua Street, past Tollitt's Bakery with her breath held to avoid the smell that pokes at her empty belly. From there she'll walk the mile and a half under the orange glow of the lamp-posts on Nelson Road and become increasingly irritated by the headlights and noise of the early traffic, turn left onto Lappet Road, left again through the cut that takes her behind the primary school and onto St. Ives Avenue. If the bedroom light is still off she will have made good time.

Mary Little removes her protective clothing, washes her hands, puts on her coat, and walks out of the Leonard & Mann office block. The air catches her breath—cold and dry like the skin between her fingers. Within five minutes she passes the bus terminal. Uniformed drivers huddle around the side door of the brick building. Her father used to do the same. He would take her there sometimes. She remembers the dark, gloss mahogany-coloured walls and the deep green wooden benches on which the drivers ate their packed lunches and sipped tea as hot as lava. The men were always loud and friendly. Big smiles greeted her and large hands patted her head. Her father missed them once he retired. For a while he used his free-for-life bus pass to travel down to the station from Marley Road. Then, one by one, his friends retired too, or they died, and the new drivers and conductors got younger and younger. Mary thinks they began to make him feel old. She imagines that the younger men didn't talk to him or, if they did, it was to poke fun. He stopped making the trip and then, eventually, stopped leaving the house. And shrivelled like a dead mouse.

A group of four drivers cross the road towards the terminal. Mary picks up the pace to avoid a collision. The sound of the bus engines rumbling in their shelters and the smell of burning diesel bring more memories. Like when she was small and thought her dad looked handsome in his uniform. And later, in her teenage years, when she grew embarrassed of it. Old and grey and loose fitting, with a cap that smelled of his oily scalp and cigarette smoke. Like a tramp, she used to think. When he was working his shift she refused to get the bus into town with the rest of her friends, preferring to walk and meet them there. She smiles a half-smile and sighs as she always does. Such nonsense. If she had a daughter, what would she think of her mother, the cleaner, in her old, once-white trainers, grey, baggy joggers and black charity shop puffer jacket?

The air is always in a hurry on Joshua Street. And she is always in its way. This morning it throws the scent of baking into her face before she can do anything to stop it. Tollitt's double doors are open but there is nothing to buy yet. A man in a short leather jacket and a woolly hat stands outside. The light from the bakery window illuminates the left side of his face, and from across the road she can see that his eyes are shut as if concentrating on the seductive smell. He is wearing a dark beard, glasses and jeans that are too tight and short for him. No socks. Just bare ankles. Three inches of white skin gleam out over his black shoes. He opens his eyes and sees her looking at him. He smiles before she can look away.

'I'm waiting to get some bread. I'm too early apparently,' he calls over to her. 'Would you like some? They should be ready soon.'

He is younger than her. Perhaps in his early thirties. He looks a little like Carlos when she first met him. He says something else but he is behind her now and the wind knocks the words away.

The direction of Joshua Street and the height of the buildings on either side make it a wind tunnel. It used to be such an untidy road. Full of boarded-up windows and rubbish piled up in every corner. But now, where there was nothing, there are bars, hotels, restaurants, florists and shoe shops, and offices that look much smarter than Leonard & Mann. Easier to clean, probably. There are flats, too—they call them loft apartments. Expensive looking. There is one, right at the end of the street, that looks as if it's made entirely from glass. Once she saw a window cleaner up there in one of those pulley contraptions they use. She wondered what he saw inside and if the people who lived there hid in the hallway until he was done like she used to when she could still afford to pay someone to clean her windows. There is a nightclub, too. Sometimes, when she's on her way to work, people are still going inside. She likes it. She doesn't scare easily, but busy streets always seem safer than empty ones.

A woman was living, or sleeping anyway, in the doorway of one of the shops for a while. Mary walked past her more times than she cares to remember. She left her food once. Just a pork pie she had in the fridge. It was going to go off anyway. She put it on the floor, as near to her as she dared, and crept away. A minute or two later she realised that the woman might not notice it, with it being wrapped in kitchen roll. So she turned back with the idea that she would say something. When she got there the woman was already eating it. She was older than Mary had expected. Probably a similar age to hers. It was difficult to know what to say so she turned around and walked away.

The lace in one of her trainers has come undone. She crouches to tie it. That's when she hears the footsteps behind her. They slow slightly, as if suddenly aware that she has noticed them, and then pick up the pace again. As they get closer, Mary braces herself. Black shiny leather brogues, bare ankles and tight dark denim calves walk past her and stop.

'Hello again,' he says. 'I thought you might like one of these.'

Is this worse than she was expecting, or better? Standing again, she can smell the bakery once more. The man has one hand in the pocket of his zipped-up leather jacket. In the other, he is holding out a brown paper bag towards her.

'No, thank you.' She forces a taut smile.

'They're fresh. Not buttered or anything, though. But that doesn't matter when they're straight out of the oven, does it?'

As the man pulls a small bread roll out of the bag, Mary pushes her hands into her jacket pockets and fumbles with her house keys.

'Are you on your way to work?'

'My husband is picking me up in a minute. I'm meeting him here.'

She is well versed in using her thumb to position the front door keys between her fingers without attracting attention to her pocket. Mary clenches her fist around the metal and notices her heart in her chest.

'That's nice of him.'

Headlights round the corner at the top of the street.

'This is probably him now,' Mary takes a step towards the curb as if fully expecting the car to stop. It drives past.

'Maybe he didn't see you. Perhaps you should have waved.'

The man stands beside her so that their shoulders almost touch. He takes another roll out of the bag and offers it to her.

'No, thank you. It wasn't him. He'll be here in a minute.'

Metal bites the skin between her fingers.

'Are you sure? They are delicious. Smell.'

He holds the bag nearer her face, but she doesn't move. Staring ahead, across the road.

'Things never taste as good as they smell.'

The man laughs.

'Yes, that's true. That's so true.'

If she'd kept walking she might have shaken him off by now. He would have realised that she wasn't going to entertain him. But now she's stuck here until he gets bored. This is why Carlos wants her to have a mobile phone.

The clacking of heels against concrete—she turns and sees a couple walking toward them. Mary looks back over to the glass apartment.

'It's nice, isn't it?'

She looks at him.

'That flat. It's nice looking. Don't you think?'

'Yes, I suppose.'

'You should see it from the inside. The view is amazing.'

The couple gets closer. They are holding hands, smiling at the man with the beard.

'Hi, Tom,' they speak in unison.

While shaking hands and kissing cheeks, all three steal glimpses of Mary.

'Good to see the pair of you. How you've been?'

'Great. A bit worse for wear at the moment, though. It's been a long night. Just heading back home now.'

As they talk, Mary steps away very slightly.

'Yeah, I'm freezing. And my feet are killing me.'

Mary looks at the woman's feet. She is wearing high-heeled sandals. Metallic. Silver, she thinks.

'Oh, yeah. I heard that you'd moved up this way.'

'Just last week. Haven't even unpacked yet. What you doing out at this time?'

'I'm just out for some air. I got some bread. Do you want some? Just out of Tollitt's oven.'

The bearded man offers the paper bag.

The woman smiles and shakes her head. Her partner takes a roll out and bites into it.

'That's just perfect.'

'Yeah, but things never taste as good as they smell,' Tom winks at Mary. The couple looks at her again. This time they smile.

The woman speaks.

'Aren't you going to introduce us?'

'I'd love to, but I don't know her name.'

They are all looking at her now.

'Mary.'

'Hi, Mary. I'm Jen and this is Matt.'

'Hello.'

'I'm just keeping her company while she waits for her husband to pick her up.'

'Always the gentleman.'

'Yeah, whatever, Jen. I must admit though, I'm getting a bit cold.

Tom looks at Mary.

'Why don't you come up to the flat and wait for your husband there? You'll see him arrive from the window.'

'That sounds like a good idea. Come on Matt, let's go home. I can't feel my legs now.'

'You two come up, too. Maggie and Jeff are there. They'd love to see you.'

'You've left Maggie with Jeff? You're a braver man than me.'

Jen nudges Matt.

'No thanks. I'd love to see them, but I really want to get home.'

She sets off and pulls Matt's hand, causing him to stumble.

'Sorry mate, maybe next time.'

'No worries. Nice to see you.'

As they walk away, Tom turns to Mary.

'Yeah, well, their loss. I'm Tom by the way.'

'Yes, I got that.'

'So, what do you think? Do want to get out of the cold for a bit?'

'No. I don't think so.'

'This is weird. I know. I'm sorry.'

'Look, I'm fine to wait here by myself. You don't have to hang around. My husband will be here any minute and he'll think it's odd that you're standing here with me.'

'Okay. Let me explain what I'm doing. Then I'll go. I live up there in that apartment. My friend—you know, Jeff who we were talking about just then—he's up there with my girlfriend. He's an old mate— haven't seen him for ages. Anyway, I was taking the piss out of him about what a crap salesman he is— he's actually really good, but it's a laugh to have a go at him, you know what I mean? He always rises to it. Hasn't changed a bit. Anyway, he got a bit annoyed at me and bet me fifty quid that I couldn't come down here and bring a stranger up from the street. I told him to get lost but he kept raising the stakes until I just had to give it a go. I was thinking, four hundred pounds to go downstairs and bring a stranger back? How hard can it be? That's why I was at the bakery before. I recognised you—I think I've seen you walking up this way a few times before. Thing is, if you come up with me I'll split the winnings with you. What do you say? Two hundred pounds just to come upstairs and say hello.'

Mary watches his face. He doesn't seem dangerous. He's quite skinny—she could flatten men twice his size when she was younger. And there was no way a man like this could be interested in her in that way. Not now anyway—not in her work clothes, smelling of bleach. And two hundred pounds. Two hundred pounds would solve a few problems.

'Like you say, it's a bit weird.' She takes another step away from him.

'Yeah, okay. I just thought I would ask. No hard feelings. Nice to meet you anyway.'

The tension drops from Mary's shoulders as Tom backs away and turns in the direction of the bakery. I'll wait until he's back down by the bakery again, she thinks, then I'll go. She looks at the road again.

'I tell you what.'

He has stopped and is facing her again.

'I'm not bothered about the money. If you come up,

you can have the lot. Four hundred pounds for coming up to the flat and saying hello. If you say no, fine. I'll go away. What do you say?'

'Four hundred pounds?'

'Yip.'

'How do I know I can trust you to give it to me?'

'I don't know. You know where I live. No, I tell you what.'

Tom unfastens his watch.

'It's an F.P. Journe. It's worth a few grand. Hold on to it. If I don't give you the money, keep it.'

Mary looks at him. All she can think is that she ought to be better at thinking things through by this stage of her life. She ought to be able to weigh up situations and assess the danger. Some kind of risk assessment.

She holds out her hand and takes the watch.

'I'm in and out, okay?'

The uniformed man behind the desk in the foyer only gives her the briefest of glances as they walk to the lifts. As they ascend, Tom speaks of how he and his girlfriend had moved from London the previous year while Mary wonders how badly she smells in a confined space. They are thinking of having children, he says. Does Mary have children? Two boys, she replies, almost whispering as if by breathing shallowly she can somehow contain the stink of her shift. Both in their twenties. No, neither of them are working. One is at college studying. The other, well, she doesn't go there.

The door to the apartment is open and another man, Jeff she presumes, is standing on the mat. His face is serious. The fire escape is the only other door in the hallway. As Tom walks towards the other man, he spreads his arms and singsongs.

'I've found someone.'

The face of the man in the doorway remains stern. He looks at Mary.

'You should leave.'

Before his words have time to register, Mary looks past him into the room that she has stared up at so many times. The giant window seems smaller from the inside and no longer appears to be one vast sheet of glass. It is actually many windows joined by thin frames. The light hits each pane differently and bounces back into the room.

Tom is speaking.

'What are you talking about, get out of the way.'

'Get back into the lift and leave. Really.'

'Stop being a dick, Jeff.'

'I can't let you do this, Tom.'

Tom looks at Mary.

'Sorry about this. He just doesn't want to lose the bet.'

'There is no bet. I'm serious. Don't come in.'

Mary starts back towards the lift.

'Mary, don't listen to him. I know what he's doing and it's out of order.'

While Tom speaks to her, Mary looks at Jeff. She is not sure but there might be a smirk appearing on his face. Nevertheless, the way he is slowly shaking his head while moving his forefinger across his throat makes up her mind. She turns, enters the elevator and hits the ground floor button with the base of her fist. As the doors begin to close, she hears the woman's voice for the first time.

'What the fuck is going on out here?'

'Jeff's being a dick, that's what.'

Mary turns just as Tom uses his arm to stop the metal lift doors closing. His face is red and his eyes large.

'Mary, get out of the lift. We have a deal or having you fucking forgotten?'

The woman pushes past Jeff and into the corridor.

She is petite and blonde, wearing a pink tracksuit and nothing on her feet.

'Leave her alone, Tom. What's the matter with you?'

'He's making me look like a fucking psychopath, that's what. This woman and I have an arrangement and Jeff is doing everything he can to make sure he fucks it up.'

The elevator doors push against his arm again.

'An arrangement? What the fuck are you up to, Tom?'

The woman pulls his arm away and looks at Mary.

'I'm sorry.'

Mary presses the button again and the doors begin to close. Tom sighs and his eyes roll upward.

'Jeff, you're a total wanker.'

As the elevator descends, Mary thinks she hears laughter but she can't be sure. It might be the mechanism as the lift lowers her away from Tom, Jeff and the woman. Tom's girlfriend, she remembers.

The wind on Joshua Street is stronger now. And colder. That's why she is shaking. She stops running when she reaches Nelson Road. After looking behind her to make sure she is not being followed, she plunges her hands into the pockets of her coat. Her knuckles push into something hard that clinks against her door keys. She pulls out the watch. The idea of returning it is only fleeting. Then her thoughts turn to Carlos. If she rushes, she might get home before he leaves for work. She'll tell him she found the watch on the ground outside the nightclub. He'll like that. He'll call her lucky.

SALT WATER

There are moments when then and now bend and buckle and collide—their contents sloshing and spilling into one another, mixing and merging—and they scramble my sense of time and place.

I am twenty-five years old, looking down at a hotplate where three breakfasts are cooking simultaneously, sizzling frantically. Spatula primed—aware of everything around me—ready to react to Dee's movements —to twist and turn and pour and serve. And I am nineteen, holding a microphone stand by its waist and neck, staring at the ground as Dee layers an intro melody over an electronic drumbeat. I will sing in a moment—just waiting—just waiting. My eyes are shut and the music creeps under my top and up my back, and I'm ready—my shoulders—my neck. This is it. The timing is explosive. It lifts us from the small stage and into the air—floating six feet up—the eyes and ears of the world are upon us. And at some point my feet are back on the ground and the music is moving around me—and through me—and out of me. We are so tight—intuitively co-ordinated, sensing where we should go next—when we should pause—how we should stop. A look, a movement, a note is all we need. Dee knows I am ready, and she holds out her hand just as I pass her a large, full English breakfast. She takes it from me without needing to look and announces it to the hungry audience.

———

I am forty-four, and warm salt water kisses my knees and pulls at an unkept promise. A woman who loves me holds my hand as we watch new friends playing with their children in the waves.

———

I am thirty, and the deep, velvety pop of the cork marks the moment my shoulders drop and my breathing slows.

No matter how much we will cry and worry for each other in the next few hours—no matter how horrified we'll become as we consider the unfairness of it all—or how much the weight of our disappointment increases—this night will be as predictable as its predecessors. We'll revel in the freedom of being able to talk—to say anything without fear of reproach or ridicule. We'll let the tears paint our cheeks with mascara as we sob like children.

Dee pours me a large glass of red wine. The sound it makes as it falls from the bottle is the signature to my times in her little flat in Murdo House. It releases many memories held captive behind the bulges of the sagging wallpaper and between the cracks in the flaking paint.

When I lived here with her, this crumbling plaster-board box had been our pauper's palace. Her eye for putting the unlikely together produced a convincing veneer of effortless style. We had nothing, but within a month, after countless trips to charity shops and late-night skip raids, Dee turned the place into a paradise. The walls were draped in huge tie-dyed fabrics and an enormous Che Guevara poster. There were two futons made from discarded pallets, and a chandelier constructed from re-engineered wine bottles hung from the ceiling. Psychedelic rugs, hand-painted crockery, framed postcards of northern seaside towns, and cushions made from the polyester superhero prints that had once adorned the chests of defiant young boys. It seemed easy—she possessed a magic spell that could transform any interior with a movement of her arm. But her powers faltered a long time ago. As our dreams gave way to compromise after compromise, her sorcery faded until there was nothing left but dust and decay. Nothing remained of the old days. The walls were bare and the cheap MDF furniture was worn and stained. Cigarette burns— thin carpets—tables piled with encrusted crockery and forgotten cassette tapes.

'I need some us-time.'

Dee placed a half-eaten plate of fried bread and baked beans onto the counter. She was back at the tables before I could answer.

'Tonight?' I asked when she returned with a tray of empty plates and mugs a few minutes later.

'Tomorrow. He's still here. Goes away in the morning.'

'Okay. You okay?'

She was off again. Customers arrived and the question wasn't answered until we'd sat down at the small red Formica table that crowded her tiny kitchen.

We always sit here, opposite each other, our heads leaning forward over a stolen pub ashtray—our intense conversations pushing our brows closer.

Secrets, if they are to be believed, need intimate proximity, hushed voices and quiet gasps. The physical closeness makes everything already known—then it's impossible to shock or embarrass.

We are two glasses in before she tears my heart from my chest and I make a promise I can't keep. I am here because she asked me to be, but also to tell her I'm ready to give up the job and my flat, and that she should do the same—that I have enough money for both of us. We could leave now—but I need to hold my tongue. She called this session, and in doing so has claimed it as hers. I have to listen first, talk later.

'He's hitting me.' There it is. Out of nowhere.

'You what?'

'He's hitting me. Dan.'

It was like a six-inch-thick slab of concrete, the length and breadth of the kitchen falling from the ceiling and smashing on the floor. The whimsical atmosphere of a second ago is now covered in grey dust.

Dee stares into the ashtray.

'When you say hitting, is this like an ongoing thing or has he just done it the once?'

'It started a few months ago. I thought it might be stress or something.'

'What happened?'

She shifts her gaze from the ashtray to the floor.

'We were arguing. Like usual. The same old stuff. Can't really remember. He'd been back for two or three days and it usually gets a bit tense. We always have a few daft fights before we get used to being around each other again, before things settle down. But they were never, you know, like physical. Well, they didn't use to be.'

'Oh, Dee.'

The last of the air in my lungs escapes in a sigh.

'I was standing in here by the cooker, and he was in the hallway. He'd been winding me up something rotten and I'd had enough. He made some other stupid comment and I… I can't even remember what I said. I just wanted it to hurt. My teeth were clenched and I sort of spat the words at him. It's not surprising, really.'

'What isn't?'

'What he did.'

'But what did he do?'

'Do you want some more wine?'

'No, I'm fine at the…'

'Hang on, I'll get another bottle.'

I watch her move to the fridge and take out a bottle. Then she bends her knees so she can pick up a fallen souvenir magnet from the floor, which she places back onto the white metal. Next, she opens a drawer. Her eyes dart from side to side as she scan its innards. Her hand goes in and starts moving things around. The sound of metal and plastic scraping against the hardboard grows louder and faster and fills the tiny kitchen with irritated noises.

'Where's the fucking corkscrew?' Her words rattle into the drawer and cause everything in it to jump and land together, smashing down so loudly I can feel them in my head.

'It's over here.'

Dee looks at me and then to my hand as I pick up the penknife-style corkscrew that rusted open years ago. She brings the bottle to the table and sits down slowly. Which is when I see the pain. The sharp upward movement of the skin over her cheekbones contorts her mouth and pushes her lower eyelids up so they half cover her eyes.

'So. So what happened?'

She sighs and takes a cigarette out of my packet.

'He just ran in here and punched me in the stomach.' She picks up a lighter and lights up. She exhales and speaks. 'I didn't even see it coming. I didn't even see him until he was right here.' She lifts her free hand and holds it six inches from her face. 'I've never been winded before. I thought I was going to die.'

I lean over and squeeze her shoulder. Our tears fall onto the red tabletop.

'It's okay. Everything is okay. We can sort this. I promise.'

We sit in silence long enough to smoke two ciga-rettes. The central heating boiler and the fridge fall silent too, and the kitchen joins our meditation. Outside there are car engines and heels on concrete pavements. Inside, my beautiful friend glows dimly as some kind of relief seems to build her up, strength-ening her mind, clearing the clouds away like a powerful warm wind. I wait until I think she's ready.

'How many times has he hit you?'

Dee exhales her smoke in short, hard bursts.

'I'm not sure now. A few. It's like, the first time—it sort of broke the seal and now it just keeps coming.'

'Dee.'

'And always in the stomach. He always punches me in the stomach.'

'It's okay. Everything is okay. We can sort this. I promise.'

I stayed with her that night. We talked until morning broke, and then we tried to sleep. I lay next to her and stared at the ceiling as a weak sun crept through the thin gap in the curtains and cut the room in two. I thought about when our lives had been easier to understand. When we had no need for hope or regret or fear. We had been giants—nothing and no one challenged us. We were magnificent. To hear our laughter, to see our swagger, to sense our majesty was to realise we were unbreakable. Inextinguishable, omnipotent, glorious. And now we were curled up on a mattress in a council flat in the arse-end of Bradford, afraid.

Her pain was my pain. I could not tolerate this situation and I vowed to get her out of it. To help her escape. Her freedom was my freedom. And as she slept and forgot the world, her beauty returned, filling her pale face, pushing away the worry lines, plumping up the dry, fading lips, and recharging her red hair. When she wakes, I'll ask her to come away with me.

———

I am eighteen and the wind blows around us, not between us.

Our lives move together—the thoughts, the words, the laughter. We are never one, but two is wrong also. There is something in between—a non-numerical expression of what lies in the space separating the single and the double—the apart and the together. We share everything we can. The money, the clothes, the music, the laughs, the terrors. We reach for objects with each other's limbs—listen with one another's ears. With her resolve and strength in the equation we are courageous. Together we are indestructible.

Me, alone, however, is a different world—a place I do everything I can to stay away from. But the shadow is always there, and sometimes while I lay awake in bed at night I stray into the darkness where my dependency hides. Because unity requires symmetry, and we are unequal. Her greater confidence, beauty and intelligence, and the fact that she must never know that I need her more than she needs me, all of this keeps us from fully joining together, of losing ourselves in one another.

————

'Are you wearing make-up?'

'Dan likes it.'

I am twenty-six and the spade plunges so deep into my chest it scrapes against my spine and scoops out my lungs. And I stand there with a chasm where there used to be a torso, feeling the remaining flesh wall collapse in on itself like wet clay. Then the words come from somewhere behind my head: I'm too late.

There was no irony in her voice. She doesn't look up. I wait for more, but there is to be no conversation. I fetch a cup of tea, and she returns to a trance that continues until the next order arrives.

I am astonished by my remarkable stupidity. By how tolerable the ache of a gut instinct becomes if ignored for long enough. By the lies I tell myself and believe. It is fine that he has taken her from my protection. He is helping me look after her. His money makes her feel good, and I benefit from her contentment. We have entered a new phase, and it's okay. We spend less time together but what we have is special. My vacating the flat so he can move in is a good thing that will see us right in the long run. If Dee is happy, I must be happy too.

————

I am twenty-five and Dan crashes into our lives in Amsterdam.

We are performing at a birthday party in return for

airfare and accommodation. It is easy for us. We don't rehearse. I read about a man who believed our physical form was made up of a limited number of layers, like an onion, and whenever a photograph was taken of you the camera stole one of these layers to create the image. If photographed enough, you would disappear. Our songs are living entities, full of finite, radioactive energy—every time we play them, they shed some of that vitality until there is nothing left but a dull, inconsequential rhythm that is barely there at all. It still exists, but not in any meaningful way. A new song is precious and alive—it has a half-life, and should not be wasted in an empty studio. So those tiny stages in the pubs and clubs are our rehearsal rooms. New tunes are worked out live—we experiment with an audience who is unaware that what they are listening to has often never been performed before.

I bring the words, Dee brings the synthesiser, and the music comes of its own accord. We sound, to our ears, incredible. Effortless togetherness has always been our way. We rarely speak about what has to be done. We never plan—everything just happens. Unquestioned and unexamined, we are twins with different parentage. Born within ten minutes and ten feet of each other, we struggled down our respective birth canals in unison. Our mothers lay in neighbouring beds in the maternity ward, which is where we began to perform—crying for milk together. Our habits drew our mothers together and the duet continued from childhood to adulthood. From Castle-port to London, and back again. Then to Amsterdam.

He insists on walking us back to our hotel. The two of them trail behind as I lead the way off Rokin and into a network of backstreets. A man stands in a doorway ahead of me. He whispers as I walk by, causing me to hesitate and look at him. He smiles and steps forward. A baseball cap pulled low, and the collar of his polo shirt high. When he puts his arm around my shoulders I shrug him off, tell him to get the fuck away from me and break into a run before turning to see where Dee and Dan are.

The man is shorter, lighter and meeker than Dan. He has spirit though and does everything he can to fight off his opponent. His actions and appearance are vicious, but the alarm in his eyes undermines the façade. He pushes a blade into the air, hissing with every thrust, and Dan laughs. Red neon bounces off the wet paving stones and up-lights the smaller man's bony features. He isn't trapped, and it's unclear why he doesn't turn and run. He lunges and Dan catches his elbow with one large hand and his extended wrist with the other. The man yelps like a small dog and the knife rattles across the concrete paving. In a blink, Dan spins him around and pulls him into his body. The angle and the darkness hide the next few seconds, but the sounds are graphic enough. Their shape moves quickly towards the nearest shop window. It shakes with the impact, and water droplets bounce and run down the glass, catching the neon as they fall. A dark mass appears at Dan's feet, which he kicks, one strike for every syllable of Dutch he spits at the floor. Black tentacles wrap around his legs but they don't slow the attack. There's a groan, a chalky whimper, and Dan is striding away, telling us to follow, the chink of his steel-tipped boots ricocheting against the walls and glass, and down the alleyway.

―――――

I am twenty-eight and I'm cleaning the zinc splash-back behind the hotplate.

The slow, repetitive wiping of the hot, soapy cloth merges with the sound of the suds as they land on hot metal, hissing and dancing until there is nothing left but tiny tendrils of steam that ripple the air—and I ease into the gentle waters of a daydream. Waves lap on the shore of a white beach, and I lay on silk cushions upon a wooden raft rising and falling over the small, frothy breakers. The sound of distant gulls. I can smell the sea at my feet and the coconut oil on my skin, and dry, hot air warms the inside of my skull. Music moves with the waves and my chest vibrates a little as I hum along, letting fragments of old lyrics escape my lips like droplets of coloured dye splashing into the clear water.

We used to talk about where we'd go. The list was endless. Every conversation added new cities and countries, festivals and beaches. Every hour's pay took us closer to our escape. Every broken yolk, over-done slice of toast, flesh burn, mug of stewed tea, dropped tomato, spilt coffee, and undercooked sausage was another step.

A year would be enough. We could work in bars and restaurants as we travelled—if there was a piano, we could even perform—we didn't need much money. Our first few airfares would be enough. But as the deadline loomed we talked ourselves into saving for another few months, and then a few more.

I don't know when she began to lose interest, but I suspect it was soon after Dan reappeared. It was a gradual thing. My enthusiasm wasn't reflected in hers quite as much. She stopped adding to the list. She spent some of her savings on a new television. I said nothing and waited for her to come round—for the romantic madness to dissolve and for her to return to me. Meanwhile, my commitment strengthened and my list grew longer.

———

The night of the revelation changed the shape of many days already passed. Moments I had previously thought of as sweet or funny now seem sinister. Like the way she used to promise me she wouldn't be late for work the morning after Dan returned from wherever he used to disappear to, but always was.

'Did you have a good night?'

'Must've done. Feel like shite.'

I'm thirty-two, and there's Dee, feeling like death in her head and in her guts, choking back the night before as she completes order slip after order slip.

'What'll it be, love?'

'Okay, darlin', take a seat. I'll bring it over when it's ready.'

'Anything to drink?'

'That'll be two-pounds-sixty, darlin'.'

She impales the completed slip onto the spike next to the hotplate. Order after order. Bang. Bang. Bang. The beat is working us, keeping us together.

And there's me, ripping the slips off the spike and adding them to the queue on the metal board in front of me; each one held in place by a magnet letter from a multicoloured alphabet. And through the steam and smoke—the sizzling and boiling—cutlery against ceramic—slurped tea and rustled newspapers—the rhythm of thirty-five men chewing with their mouths open—I watch her and imagine a time when she might suffer like that for me.

———

I am forty-four and I can still describe her as if she were standing in front of me in a dream. But to think of him is like scraping my knuckles against a brick wall.

She was electrifying—the power behind every positive thing that happened to us. The gigs, the jobs, and all the little breaks that came our way were all generated by her. Wherever we went, people wanted to help us (her), give us (her) a hand up, and to assist us (her) on our (her) way. She demanded more than attention—there was something about her that forced others to help her. She entered their consciousness via their hearts as well as their eyes. Men and women made personal sacrifices, large and small, so that they could be of service to her. They gave her gifts, advice and time. Strangers offered her meals, places to stay, money and lifts to destinations far out of their way. Casual acquaintances thought of her while they shopped, or as they cleared their lofts, and brought her things she might find useful. By her mid-twenties, she was the beneficiary of more kindness than any one person could reasonably expect during a lifetime. And she glided through all of it, unaware of the effect she had.

She was physically beautiful—but people were fascinated by more than her outward appearance. It was something deeper, hidden behind her small, pale, orange-freckled, mischievous face, electric, effervescent eyes, and tiny facial expressions that never repeated themselves. Or perhaps it hid in her neck—which, when her hair was tied back, looked thicker and longer than she needed—in one of those fine, pink creases that vanished when she lifted her head to laugh. Or was it buried inside her long slender torso—or somewhere along the deep ravine that ran down her back—or just below the surface of that soft, wide tummy—or just beyond the breasts that pushed out a little too far—or on the far side of the full backside—or at the end of her lengthy and perfectly formed legs with their porcelain calves that winked at you when she walked? But by far the most natural place for it to conceal itself was in her hair. A wild, red volcano of wiry curls—out of proportion and permanently moulting, chucking out never-ending strands of lava. Wherever it hid, it was present in the way she laughed, sat down, washed up, ate, crossed her legs, blew her nose, folded her clothes, walked upstairs, yawned, slept—a profoundly beautiful something that ran through everything she did. I never tired of watching her, and I wasn't alone—all eyes gravitated to Dee.

She had grace—the likes of which I have never known again. She was goodness and dignity in flesh and bone. This was evident in her moral judgement and sense of injustice, both of which were tuned far higher than average. And that is how she gave back. There were many times in our lives together when incidents that I would have walked past stopped her in her tracks. And there she stayed until good prevailed. She argued with adamant teachers, belligerent police officers, angry, drunken men, and proud mothers—and she would apply force or charm or volume or sickening sweetness or sheer strength of will until she got the compromise, apology or recompense she believed was deserved. She was arrested once, punched in the face twice, and wrestled to the floor by an overweight taxi driver, all in the name of justice. I was always there—right behind her, watching her back—nodding and repeating whatever she said—taking the knocks, dodging the missiles, and wiping the blood from her nose.

I tried to explain all of this to her once. While other businesses around us were failing, the café was always busy and its popularity seemed to be increasing. I said it was down to her, and I did my best to describe what I meant. She laughed, paused, shook her head, and laughed again. She said I was being silly. But I could tell she understood—she always did. Just as I understood I needed her beauty and her grace. Her bloody-mindedness and her short temper, her strength and her power—all of these things were vital to my survival.

He was a negative force. He sapped energy from situations—killed them by proximity. He was empty. Barren, like a post-demolition wasteland. A wrecking ball head, cropped dark hair and a North Sea complexion. He believed it was acceptable to bring up phlegm whenever and wherever, and preferred to empty his nose by pressing a gnawed finger to one nostril and blowing hard. A farting, ball-scratching Neanderthal who was more comfortable with his mouth hanging open than closed.

Every new person was a possible victim. Another's misfortune was a possible angle. Scheming with the subtlety and empathy of a hungry dog, he took his chances without a thought for anything around him. We knew he was a crook. It was never hidden from us. We laughed about his escapades. I'd ask how he was doing, and Dee would roll her eyes, and say: 'You'll never guess what he's been up to,' and the story of a new misadventure would follow.

Once, her phone pinged with a text message while we were in the middle of a rush. She shook her head, dialled a number, wedged the phone between her right shoulder and jaw, and reported her car stolen while she changed the till roll. There was no explanation—just a slightly embarrassed smile.

I never questioned her alliance with someone who broke the law. The heightened sense of injustice I so admired her for had never been guided by the law of the land. Her fury at unfairness had been directed towards the police on more than one occasion. So, morally there was no conflict about getting intimate with someone who showered her with clothes and jewellery and handbags—all of which we assumed stolen, and most of which she shared with me. We painted him as a modern-day Robin Hood, fighting the corruption of the system and distributing his spoils amongst the poor.

'The perks of harbouring a gangster.'

However, the real reason why I didn't question the partnership was that she had fallen in love with him —there was nothing I could do except hope it would end soon. Love can ignore a legion of warning signs— the forged passports she found hidden under the bedroom carpet—the whispered telephone calls in the middle of the night—the cuts on his knuckles and the blood on his clothes—and the long, unexplained absences. Love also cuts friends adrift if they threaten the newly found happiness, which was something I could not allow to happen. So I laughed at the stories, accepted my share of the loot, and waited for sanity to return.

———

I am thirty-eight and it has taken me twenty-five minutes to find the courage to knock on the door of the flat.

Dan opens it, tuts and disappears back into the darkness of the hallway, leaving the door ajar. I wait for a moment then enter.

Dee is in their bedroom. She has packed his clothes into a large, black holdall. The noise of the TV in the adjoining room floods through the thin walls and muffles my approach.

Her hug is tight and long. After releasing me, she signals I should be quiet and points to the chair in the corner of the room. I remove the clothes from it and sit down. She looks better than I had expected. There are no marks on her face and she doesn't shake. When she's finished, she zips up the bag, drags it out of the bedroom and closes the door. I hear her take it to the front door and then walk into the living room. There is no audible reaction when she tells him his bag is ready.

It is a wildlife documentary. A hushed voice describes the habitat of a primate. I open the bedroom door and creep into the hallway. The door to the living room is open slightly and I can see them sitting next to each other on the sofa through the thin strip of light below the hinge.

'Do you want a cuppa before you go?'

'What do you fucking think?'

She gets back on her feet and walks to the kitchen. Dan lights a cigarette with the flame of an oversized Zippo; the leaves of a green marijuana emblem poke through his fingers. Tattoos of various designs and standards crawl out from beneath his tight black vest, stretching over his shoulders and flabby biceps, all the way down to his vein-marbled knuckles. From the neck of his vest another design writhes up behind his left ear, like a thick, black vapour. On his extended, crossed legs he wears black tracksuit bottoms, and black flip-flops on his pale feet.

When he sucks on the cigarette, his entire face contorts towards his small, pinched mouth, from which lines radiate out like a dying star. He exhales a thin grey plume of smoke, pushing it down towards the floor where it mushrooms and sinks into the old floral carpet. Without taking his eyes from the television, he swings his arm to the right like a tower crane, lowering it to the cushion and wrapping his fingers around a thick glass ashtray, which he places on his stomach. And when he brings up the other hand to flick the cigarette, I catch a glimpse of the dark red demon in the throes of laughter on the underside of the forearm. Intense, yellow eyes peer out from a menagerie of dragons and coiled serpents and Aztec gods. Each time he lifts the cigarette back to the ashtray, the red face stares out at me—looking me straight in the eyes—goading me—like these are

Dan's actual eyes, the reason why he doesn't need to look about him to find the ashtray—the eyes he uses to watch me. I retreat to the bedroom and wait for him to leave.

'Won't you miss your train?' Dee's voice wakes me. Shadows shuffle in the gap at the bottom of the door.

'You'd like that, wouldn't you?' Dan's dirty laugh stops short and I imagine them kissing.

He, squeezing her arse.

She, willing him out of the door.

She breathes.

'Yeah, of course. But I'm just worried about you getting into trouble.'

'They don't need me there until the morning so I thought I'd catch a later one.'

The front door opens.

'Oh.'

'What do you mean, "Oh"?'

'Nothing.' Her voice an octave higher. 'It's nothing. I just thought yesterday you said something about not wanting to be late.'

The pause is too long.

'Yeah, but that was before I got the call.'

'Oh, okay. I just didn't hear you get a call. Well, you take care of...'

'So I'm a fucking liar, am I?'

'No, I didn't mean anything. I just...'

'No, of course you didn't mean anything. You never mean anything because you're too fucking stupid to mean anything.'

It sounds like a clap with a deep echo.

'Idiot.'

The door slams shut.

From the living room window I watch him walk past the closed shop fronts and towards the car park, talking on his mobile phone. From up here he looks harmless. I squash him with my thumb against the pane.

Dee sobs into a cushion.

'Fucking bastard, fucking bastard.'

He stops and drops his bag. He walks around it as he speaks into one hand. The other hand lifts into the air and falls as the demon scans the building. Up and down it goes in tiny exaggerated movements like he's conducting the rows of parked cars. He points at the air in front of him and then pushes his palm against the side of his face.

My focus glazes. Today is not the day to tell her I am leaving.

———

He returns, she drinks and she obeys.

He leaves, she drinks and she heals.

She, always pleased to see him walk through the door.

He, happy to be home with his girl.

She, maybe it'll be better this time.

He, I didn't mean it last time, I was under a lot of pressure.

She, he doesn't mean it, he's under a lot of pressure.

He, it's so good to be home.

She, he's making a real effort.

He, why is my dinner cold?

She, shit, I've fucked up.

He, what have I told you about keeping my food hot?

She, I'm sorry, let me put it in the microwave.

He, you're sorry? I can't eat sorry, can I? I've been

risking my arse for you, and you can't even serve me a hot fucking meal?'

———

She replied to my first text. I had wanted her to know she couldn't expect me to put my life on hold while she wasted hers. I wanted to beg her to come with me. Instead, I told her I was leaving and didn't know when I would be back. Pressing send was like cutting an old rope with a sharp new knife, and her response was the sound of the cords hitting the floor.

Are you fucking joking?

I am 39, and I still send her things. Small envelopes, padded packets, and boxes. Whenever I find something I think will help her—gifts, ideas, advice, anything that might put a smile on her face or some hope in her heart—I take it, package it and get it to her as quickly as I can. Little envoys of love and happiness I kiss before posting. I want her heart to flutter as the postman walks into the café with another parcel with a foreign stamp under his arm— another tiny gem of intrigue, mystery and excitement.

Some of the things I've sent to her:

—a poem I ripped from a book in a Barcelona library.

—boxes of chocolates I stole from the best confectioners in Antwerp,

—an irresistible old postcard of two sisters skipping and holding hands from a dilapidated Bordeaux brocante,

—three outrageously expensive perfumes I lifted in LA,

—a napkin from a desert roadside café called Dee's Diner,

—a mixtape of Mexican pop made for me by a boy in Toluca de Lerdo,

—a pressed yellow flower (I don't know its name) from my landlady's collection in Quito,

—an old silver ring with an empty setting I found on the grass in Maruyama Park,

—a selection of thin, metal cogs from a toy car I couldn't fix for an elderly man who sat next to me on a bus journey to Datong,

—a shopping list with a love heart drawn at the bottom, which I found in a supermarket car park in Nagoya,

—a carved wooden whale I found on a beach in Macau.

———

I am about to turn forty-one and the sun is shining on Castleport.

I lean against a metre-wide, planted-up, concrete tube opposite the entrance to Murdo House, and look up at Dee's windows eleven floors up, and wait.

Murdo House is one of three tower blocks joined at their bases by a large, self-contained, shopping precinct. This giant construction was once somebody's vision of a future that never arrived. A place containing everything a community required—a discount supermarket, cheap fast food outlets, a post office, a job centre and a wide selection of betting shops, all interspersed with a smattering of vacant units with photographs of thriving greengroceries and bakeries mounted on their boarded fronts. In the middle is a large pedestrianised area which, when the sun shines, has a relaxed and un-British air. Children clamber and chase each other over a small mound of concrete U-shapes—an avant-garde climbing frame that looks like a miniature sixties' castle. Shoppers meander between retailers, crisscrossing the northern piazza, laden with carrier bags and trolleys. Sun cream, sweat, and cigarette smoke fill the air. Pensioners in heavy coats keep to the shaded shop fronts, planning their routes via the shadows cast by the decorative roof bridges that stitch the two sides of the precinct together.

I don't have to wait for long. She skips through the

open doors of the flats looking brighter than the rays that bake the paving stones her sandalled feet slap against. In sunglasses, a white baggy t-shirt and tight jeans, she turns right and walks with her fingers pushed into her trouser pockets. The outline of her red hair blazes as she moves. My stomach twists tightly, and I rise from my seat to catch her. After only a few paces she stops to speak to a man. They seem happy to see each other. She places a hand on his shoulder and kisses his cheek. I stop to watch the interaction.

He is telling her something, and she beams.

'That's brilliant... happy for you... how long are you back for?'

'...couple of days... see mum...'

'I saw her just yest... seems better... it must be...'

'...it is... not easy...'

Feeling self-conscious, I retreat to the nearest wall and lean against it.

She keeps standing back to take him in, like a mother seeing her son in uniform for the first time. He is younger and I imagine she knew him as a small child —perhaps she was friends his mother or older sister. It's good to see her finding pleasure in talking to this man.

The pair have been talking and smiling for ten

minutes when I notice a quick movement in the corner of my eye. A dark shape hurtles towards them from the left and within seconds it is upon them. I don't recognise him at first. He seems fatter than the last time I saw him, and his hair is shoulder-length and wild. His mouth is smiling, but his eyes are aflame. He moves fluidly and fast. The fist he uses to punch the side of Dee's head opens and grabs the arm she raises to shield herself from the next attack, while he extends the index finger of his other hand towards the young man's face. Then he parts his thin, smiling lips and, through teeth that are clenched so tightly it looks as if his jaw might explode, he fires rounds of words into her right ear.

'Where. The. Fuck. Is. My. Milk?'

With each word he yanks her nearer to him and the smile grows larger.

'All. I. Want. Is. A. Cup. Of. Fuck. Ing. Tea!'

Every syllable marks another movement back towards the doors of Murdo House.

'Is. That. Too. Much. To. Fucking.'

The second punch lands on the same side of her head.

'Ask?'

The young man doesn't move. And except for a handful of older residents who stop to stare, the shoppers continue on their way, glancing at the couple out of the corners of their eyes, wishing they would take their problems indoors.

Then it is over. The pair disappears through the revolving glass door. A teenage girl looks over her shoulder as she exits the building, and walks away with a furrowed brow.

The young man sucks in his bottom lip. He takes two steps towards the entrance, glances at his mobile phone and looks around for someone to tell him what to do next. But the witnesses have moved on. There is no echo in the air and no blood on the floor. He shakes his head, puts the phone in his pocket, turns and leaves.

———

I am forty-three and I see Mira for the first time. We are in a cafe on the other side of Europe. It is the cheapest place I could find with a view of the river. I sit at a small table at the back next to a window, nursing a strong coffee and a piece of sweet, moist cake, and study a map of Budapest I picked up at the train station.

It's her laugh that catches my attention. It explodes from the behind the counter, like a water balloon hitting the side of my head. I am the only person to look up.

A slim woman who looks a little younger than me is shaking her head and beaming a smile through a large gap between her two front teeth. Her dark hair —short and sculpted into a quiff that pointed up at the end—is as striking as her laughter. She wears a brown apron over a vest, and her lean, muscular shoulders and arms flex as she leans her weight onto the counter. She pulls her smile down and turns in my direction, a faint smirk still emanating. Her large brown eyes meet mine and she releases a little more of her smile for me.

It is a fast romance. That night I sleep on her sofa, and when I wake up I find her next to me, my arms are around her.

The morning we spend exploring her neighbourhood. She shows me her old school and introduces me to the old women who sit under the shade of the park trees. We eat pancakes and drink coffee and talk like express trains.

She says I am good for her English.

Some days I call in at the cafe an hour before she finishes. I study her. The flicks of her head that remove an imaginary fringe from her face—the unselfconscious pinch of her top lip between thumb and forefinger—the way, when standing at the espresso machine, she tilts her head to the right and lets her gaze disconnect from her mind so she can be elsewhere for a moment. And as I watch, her beauty appears to me in new ways. There is majesty in the minutiae, the way she accommodates the tiny, unspoken needs of those around her. My smile aches as Lila, one of the women she works with, pats her apron pockets and turns to find a pen so she can write a new order, only to find Mira already holding one out to her—as she speaks to a familiar customer about the weather, she glides to the door without taking her eyes off him and opens it so another man, laden with boxes, can enter—when two new arrivals get to their table, she leans over them and places a teaspoon next to each of their cups before they realise they need them. And there are more of these, many more. It's as if she is tuned into every being, ignoring nothing—profoundly alert. She never waits for an acknowledgement, just moves onto the next micro-scopic problem to be solved, nanoseconds before it occurs.

That's why I don't have to ask her to come with me. She packs a rucksack and tells me it is time to go.

––––––

I am forty-one and I still dream about Murdo House.

It is always the same. Nighttime, and I am standing in the concrete precinct. The air is illuminated by explosions of light from the hundreds of windows that overlook me—the colours and sounds of hard-lived lives swirl and dance above my head. They mushroom and snowball out of the rectangular holes, working to their own patterns and tunes, but occasionally fall into line, like a reprieve in a deranged jazz solo. It's a melody of suffering and unhappiness that is so intense that every cell in my body tries to drag me away from the building before I am overwhelmed. But the silence from the eleventh-floor windows keeps me there—the windows of Dee's flat are like the eyes of a corpse.

I enter through the communal door and walk from one end of the flickering foyer to the other, past a group of five hooded teenage boys, leaning against a wall, looking straight ahead, saying nothing. The lift is filthy. I pull my sleeve over my hand before I press elevator button with a covered knuckle. As the doors judder shut, a cloud of bleach and urine vapours wraps itself around me and I bring my sleeve to my face.

Every time the electronic red digits disappear and reappear, counting my ascent on the little screen above the console, the dim fluorescent tube behind a metal-grilled ceiling flickers off and on again. The higher I am hoisted, the longer the darkness seems to stay.

The light from the corridor scratches at my corneas

and lifts the graffiti off the wall so that it floats—hovering over the cream, textured plasterboard, wrapping itself around a tunnel of old air. I follow the lines and shapes towards Dee's flat.

The door is open and I walk into dense darkness. But as I move into the flat, I pass through the blackness and out of the other side. When I turn, I can barely see the door despite there being enough light to illuminate everything else in the hallway. My hand disappears at the wrist as I push it back into the shadow. There is a physicality to it—lukewarm liquid, lighter than water. I grip my fist and withdraw, expecting to be holding a handful of shadow in my hand.

There are several men in the living room. Dan is sitting on the sofa, looking at his bare feet on the floor. Everyone else is searching cupboards and drawers, but the shadow I found in the hallway is in these places too. I see it in the periphery of my vision—shapes that disappear when I try to focus on them. It's as if it is aware of us, following us as we search for clues. When one of the men opens a drawer in the dresser next to me, the contents inside plunge into darkness. Wherever they point their attention, the light is removed.

These men begin to enter the dark kitchen. It is small in there, so I wait for them to return but they don't come back. Although I know what is coming, I walk through the doorway and try to pass through the darkness just as I did in the hallway. This time there is no light at the other end. People are shouting and begging for help. Somebody grabs at my clothes and I panic.

———————

I am thirty-two and I stand on my tiptoes so I can peer over the splashback and the three-quarter wall, and into the giant soup of diners—three tables wide and five deep.

Sometimes, between orders, I look to see who is there, and I find a familiar stranger to fill the moment with a new story. The weakened natural light that survives the journey through the road-dirty window brightens the faces of the diners on the first two tables it reaches before it dies of exhaustion. It illuminates their features in such gentle colours that these work-weary men, with their hard brows and tired eyes and skin, have, for the moment, the countenance of boys—of angels. Their still expressions tell stories of love and innocence and adventure. But the mood to their right is darker. The fluorescent strips that line the polystyrene-tiled ceiling have the opposite effect of the refined glow from the window. If I stare for long enough, the blue-white ray mutates everyone it touches, melting skin with science fiction-strength radiation. The further from the window I look, the more abnormal the faces grow until I reach the rasping white wall at the opposite side of the room where I only find stories of shipwrecks, cold and dead.

This is where we are—marooned by a roundabout, taking shelter behind a till, a hotplate and a tea urn, lifetimes away from our dreams. Somehow, somewhere we drifted off course and sailed further from a destination that once seemed inevitable. One of the storms we have weathered must have damaged the rudder or torn the sails.

———

I am forty-four and the hand holding mine belongs to Mira. The children who laugh as the waves tickle their backs belong to a couple we met at the hotel. The warm salt water that kisses my knees belongs to the Pacific. If I stand here for long enough the brine may erode the colliding memories and, perhaps, an unkept promise will float away.

LOST CARGO

A light, cool gust falls into the room and licks the soles of his feet, melts into his bare legs and back, and grants him a brief moment of heaven—the first relief since the door of the aeroplane opened and he inhaled the Catalonian air. Air: a substance commonly associated with a particular concoction of gases, one of which should most certainly be oxygen. But there is none of that precious stuff here. The people in this city breathe hot syrup.

Since his arrival, the minutes and hours have folded in on themselves. Face down and naked on this bed— the city has collapsed and fallen into hell. How else could he explain this disorientation—this heat. He imagined flames licking the walls of the hotel, and people everywhere writhing in muted agony.

Things began to go wrong when the wheels of the plane left the Castleport tarmac. That was the moment he was hit by the slab of nausea. It had felt as if the gravitational force dislodged an internal organ, which then slipped between two others, like one bucket of dead fish being poured into another. From that point, coherence has been unwinding itself and the fever has been closing in. Throughout the flight—his first, and at the present rate of deterioration his last—only the thought of alighting and breathing real, unprocessed air eased the howls from his guts. And with closed eyes and the side of his head resting against the plastic innards of the plane, he imagined the air's healing properties on the edge of his nostrils, sweet and fresh, filling his body with goodness and light. It would inflate him like a balloon and push everything back into place, and all would be right again. This was when he was sure he'd survive —before he'd descended the stairs to the runway and his lungs rejected the hot, dense air with a startled cough—before he looked to his fellow passengers in disbelief but instead of shock saw lowered brows and small, impatient eyes that nudged him deeper into the invisible soup—and before, exhausted, he opened his mouth and let the heat pour into him.

———

A mattress spring is digging into his ribs. He tries to

twist his spine a little in an attempt to move but fails. He'll try again later. He'll need to get up soon, anyway, to find something to moisten his pumice tongue. Don't touch the tap water, mind. That's what she said. She's been abroad. Knows that kind of thing. Don't drink it. It'll give you the shits, so it will. But this is no longer enough of a deterrent. There are probably seven steps to the bathroom. More like seven mountains. Seven Sahara deserts. Seven black-holes. For the time being he extends his lips and lets a cool, imaginary liquid fill his mouth, wash the taste of his guts away, and roll down his throat like the Stride Falls.

This was all her idea. Rachael. She went away by herself once—when she was younger. Tenerife. Ten-er-eefee. She met a local and fell in love for a week. Eleven years later and she still talks about it. Although to be fair, the romance has only leaked into conversation thirty-odd times since they got together. Maybe forty, but who's counting? But she's good for him. They'd only been going out for a few months before his dad died. She's been like a rock, she has. Go somewhere, she said. Get away for a weekend. Do one of those weekend breaks.

Did you have a good flight?

He remembers two large, moist eyes jabbing at him from the rearview mirror. A flame-shaped, cardboard air freshener danced below, coating the edges of the vacuum with a slick of perfume. The taxi driver, a man uncomfortable with silences, talked, whistled and tapped the dashboard to the beat of the indicators—anything to occupy the emptiness left by his pallid, shivering passenger. Like a boiling egg, the crown of the driver's beige, bald head jiggled as he threw accent-laden queries over his shoulder. The notion that, as a passenger, his monosyllabic responses might cause offence flitted by like a bat— but the questions were unbearable. All he could do was pray for somewhere to lie down—to beg for the buildings and roads and cars to melt away so he could be delivered to the hotel quickly before the driver questioned him to death. Were it not for the seat belt he would have crumpled and, possibly, mercifully, expired on that back seat. But instead, eventually, he reached this sweat-damp hotel mattress from where he now edits and replays the lop-sided conversation in his fever-ridden imagination, revising his grunts and sighs with better replies.

Did I have a good flight? Oh, aye. It was magic, man. And don't be fooled by my ashen skin colour and profuse sweat. These are merely the result of having enjoyed myself far too much at such high altitudes. Reckless of me, really. Cham-

pagne, charlie and a couple of stewardesses. This raging fever is nothing more than a mile-high playboy hangover. Did I have a good flight? Damn right.

The hot air has cauterised his saliva glands and his tongue hunts in crevices for moisture. Little secretions appear in unlikely places—on the crumbling roof of his mouth, on the bed sheet next to his lips—but they evaporate before they reach his throat. A drop of water is all he wants in the whole world. Did he buy a bottle at the airport? Didn't he put it into his... his bag! Where is it? Did he collect it at the airport? Shit, shit, shit. It's got everything in it. What's he going to do? How the hell is he going to get it? More pain. Eyes wide open now. He left it at the airport. Or the taxi. Or in the street as he staggered from the cab to the hotel. Or... it doesn't matter where. It's gone and so has he. He's never getting home now. Cooked alive in an oven with a balcony. And before his eyes can force themselves shut again, he scans the floor for a sign of hope. The arm of a white polo shirt, the soiled toe of a Converse. His phone. Rachael. She could have explained things better. The heat. Why didn't she tell him about the heat? And what to do if he got sick. He should call her.

The light is fading. It might be the sun setting on

Barcelona. Or just on him. The oxygen in his blood has finally run out. Drowning is supposed to feel good—he remembers from somewhere—once you succumb to the inevitable and let the water in. And it does. Yes, this is it. Adios, grassy arse. Nice knowing you. Time to pay the maker a wee visit. Or it would be, but dying isn't easy when the man next door is barking senseless noises, impossible to block. Ignorant bastard. Doesn't he realise there's a visitor to his country just a few feet away trying to perish in peace? Show some respect. Have a bit of common decency, please. But Big Voice increases in size and splashes into the watery delirium. And this vocal thunder— this undersea earthquake that shakes the foundations of the hotel—is not alone. Under the sub-aquatic acoustics there is a woman too. Quieter. More cautious. Every time she squeaks, Big Voice smashes her words to pieces, like a bear stamping on a mouse —mashed vowels oozing between its toes. So loud. With his eyes closed, it's as if the source is kneeling by his bed, growling into his face. These walls are cheap and paper-thin. The owner of vocal cords like those could easily come crashing into his room by resting his weight against it. White vest tucked into dark, tight jeans. Hairy shoulders and a bald spot. Lying on the floor, covered with a fine layer of plaster, the perplexed and angry man would turn to him and shout, 'Are you on holiday?' Who, me? Well, let's have a look and see, shall we? Let's have a little shifty. Falling in and out of consciousness, check.

Hallucinating so convincingly that the world appears to be wrapped in black metallic paper, check. Occasionally convinced that my dead dad is out in the street, shouting my name and laughing at me—pissing himself at the mess I'm in, double check. The sod knows fine well this is his fault. If he hadn't gone and died there wouldn't have been any cash to waste on a trip. He'd never have spent good money on going abroad, that's for sure. Full of foreign muck. Should've listened to him—not to Rachael and her stupid ideas. Pretentious cow. Take some time off, she said. See some of the world. Go sweat to death in a cheap hotel room in Barcefuckinglona. Yeah, sounds like a grand idea. Yeah, lose all your things on the way, too, like your passport and wallet and stuff. Aye, that'll be magic—let's do it. So yeah, I am on holiday. Living the dream, you might say. Living the dream.

Big Voice is quiet now and the woman is speaking. Those soft, high-pitched tones scamper and then pause, and wait for danger. Then, satisfied the coast is clear, off they go again, scurrying to the nearest table leg or crack in the skirting board. The cadence transports the deathly eavesdropper to the minutes before he found his room—to the hotel corridor and the smiling woman. There had been nothing behind that smile, though. Of course, of course. After all, she was watching a corpse drag itself along the corridor of a cheap hotel. Stumbling and jarring his shoulder against a doorframe, and then pushing the left side of his body along the wall, lifting briefly to avoid another collision. A fly buzzed around him. He saw her feet first. Trainers. Blue Nikes, tightly fastened with bright white laces. No order to them. Like smashed teeth, gnashing at the brown skin that bridged the gap between shoe and clingfilm-tight jeans. Turn-ups, at least six inches high. Mental-looking things. And the carpet! Thin maroon stripes juddering like an old video game. On any other day he'd have laughed at the way the floor moved beneath those feet, but there wasn't so much as a smirk left inside of him. Just a hard, shrivelled lump that rattled as he bounced off the walls. If he was ever going to get to his room, he realised, he'd need to navigate around these sockless ankles. It was only then he grasped the fact that these feet belonged to a person. As he lifted his head, everything between the shoes and the uncertain, smiling face passed in a blur, and his brain spun behind his eyes like a fruit machine. He noticed the redness around her cheekbones first, and then her eyebrows, deep, black and fast. Hair tied back, with a side parting which cut into her scalp. Possibly attractive but it was difficult to tell. And then, that pained smile for a sweating tourist who slithered along the corridor, leaving a trail of mucus. She opened her mouth and words fell out, most of them hit the ground before reaching his ears. He tried to move out of her way but fell back against the wall. She spoke again. Her words were smooth and meaningless. And then, in the time it took to close and open his eyes, too slowly to qualify as a blink, she was gone.

Where am I from? Now then, there's a question. Good one. Pertinent, you might say. You know what, though? I'm not sure. I'm not sure I'm from anywhere. Perhaps—and I think this might be true—I have always been in the back of this cab, with my cranium vibrating against the window, like a sickly, beak-less woodpecker—gulping at the hot syrup to keep my stomach muscles calm—quietly fighting against those bitter, bulbous tones of your heavy accent that pound my eyes closer and closer together until, eventually, if I'm not careful, you smash them into a single sphere. This could be where I'm from, though, couldn't it? I've been here all along.

Up there, somewhere in the unfathomable distance, the last waves throw back their great heads and collapse onto the moonless surface—the final white froths fizz and fade until there is silence. Vague, grey light scratches at the dark, salty dermis with blunted claws and broken fingernails, and fails to make a mark. Deeper, and closer, where the limbless crabs and the dead fish, with barnacled plastic soldiers in their bellies, neither float nor sink—deeper still, through the disembodied limbs of ice-cold kelp that appear and disappear like phantoms, and into the skull-crushing depths where his darkest moments hide behind shipwrecks and serpents. This is where he lies. On a mattress that is eating him. Dissolving him slowly. His chest and right cheek have already been digested. Legs, too. He is lying on the tongue of a leviathan—sinking into the stomach lining of a whale. Swallowed whole. The stench of his own fluids mixing with the creature's juices is comforting, and his impatience is soothed by the certainty that soon all of this will be over. Liquefied and liberated. Free to explore the cool oceans among the cells of this enormous beast. Together they will dive deep into the dark depths of the earth and beyond, free from sickness and pain. The rapture of the deep. Blackness behind his eyes darkens and soon everything will be shed. Left with nothing but his shadow, he will traverse the seabed, out of reach of the longest fingers and sharpest stares. Protected by this viscid water, this soft, sandy floor. A lost cargo—an old leather suitcase, adhesive disintegrating, his name and his past abraded and torn by the salt.

And as he swims through slitted eyelids, there are shouts from the search party on the other side of the mammal's flesh. They will never find him in here. It's too late now. Anxious, angry voices—eager to locate the foreigner lost under the sea—frustrated by the futility. There is nothing that can be done. He tries to respond, to fill his lungs, but his mouth and throat have gone the way of his chest. He thinks as loudly as he can: it's too late.

The great whale dives and he spins slowly—legs rising, head falling, around he goes, again and again. All about him, wreckage and empty treasure chests, corpses and shoes, rags and fragments of photographs that hang amongst the seaweed and scaly carcasses in the wash of the cetacean's warm acid. But voices still pursue him—clinging onto the dorsal fin, sobbing for him. She has followed him down here. It's too late. Surely she must realise? No hope for him now. Urgent, desperate, meaningless words float up to the surface and away. A door clatters in its frame and a scream harpoons his dream. He lifts his head from the bed. A cry, footsteps, a distant door slams. There is little to see—a grainy dullness with occasional calcium highlights—the bones of fellow seafarers.

———

The water at his feet is as brown as tea as three days' worth of stale, crusted sweat dissolves and washes down the plughole. Under the cool shower, the situation seems more manageable than it did a few minutes ago when he sat on the edge of the bed, waiting for his phone to charge so he could find out what time it was—and what day it was. He can't think straight with a seventy-hour hunger in his belly, but he can handle the basic stuff. His plane leaves in four and a half hours. Soon, he will get out of the shower and dry himself. Then, he will attempt to clean the room, but there is only so much you can achieve with a fistful of cheap toilet paper. Once he has dressed and has repacked a rucksack he has no recollection of believing lost, he will go out and find food. He has money, so it can't be that difficult. Someone will speak English. Rachael said.

The water fills his ears, and his mouth makes a cave behind the cascade. He feels cleansed, as if he has sweated, shat and puked away all the dark clouds. He can even think of his dad without his stomach contracting like a fist. He pictures him, looking down, calling him a thick twat—saying only he could be stupid enough to sleep through an entire holiday— but it leaves no mark.

With a towel wrapped around his waist, he stands at the open balcony door. The warmth of the sun dries his skin, making it feel tight and smooth. It's as if it fits properly for the first time. The rays nourish him in a way he's never experienced before, and his confidence lifts. Below, a wide pedestrian area is sand-wiched between two narrow roads. Treetops and, below them, tired, branded parasols obscure much of his view of the ground, but he can see, a little further along to the right, hundreds of people drifting through the warmth. From here they look young and healthy—a lifetime of sunshine paying dividends. Rachael said this road stretches all the way to the sea, and he senses that now—it's as if the people are tidal, ebbing and flowing over the paving stones every few minutes. There is music too, which he realises he has been able to hear since he woke up. A man sits on a small amplifier, with a black guitar flopped on the lap of a folded leg. His head moves from side to side as he plays a vaguely familiar tune—black, slack curls sweeping to and fro.

In the taxi, he reverses a journey he can barely remember. The driver is quiet, so he gazes out of the gaping window as the car inches through the city. People sitting at outdoor cafes, drinking and laughing —mottled shade from a bright green canopy—shards of sunlight illuminating heads and shoulders— ancient, ornate lampposts—an old man beams as he embraces a young woman—sunshine on aluminium chairs. He sucks it all in through hungry eyes. As they pass a long line of parked mopeds, he looks up at the windows of the buildings, five floors of closed shutters. All life is down here. Down here with the flaking trees and red-rimmed kiosks and potted plants. Sure-footed people materialise between the slow-moving vehicles, while others, squinting, emerge from sunken escalators—and the taxi rolls towards a wider street and palm trees and pillars of ripped posters. They swerve right and soon the road opens up and the traffic accelerates, and the arches of Barcelona disappear.

THE TEARS OF NOEL HARDY

Noel Hardy woke, reached to his left and confirmed his suspicion that he was alone in bed. The en suite light was off. He remained motionless, his breathing shallow and quiet, but he could hear nothing from the house. As he listened, he felt his body pressing into the mattress—his back first, then his shoulders, pelvis and legs. He imagined he was sinking deeper into the foam, its form taking on more of his, his head submerging further into his pillow until the white linen touched his cheekbones. And when he could descend no further, his focus turned to the dim outline of the ceiling rose—like a hole through which the sounds from outside fell into his large, dark bedroom. A car drove past the house, grinding loose gravel into tarmac—further away, someone took irregular steps, pausing, and walking again—the humming of yellow streetlights—oak leaves scratched and tapped one another as a wind limped through the park—the threads of a web strummed under a spider's tread. The sounds dropped through the hole and filled the room with a faint fog that seemed to amplify the silence of the house. It was a silence that meant Mary was no longer with him at Treetops, and Hardy began to cry.

———

Nurse Andrea moved forward with well-rehearsed steps, taking care not to tread on the feet and ankles of the patients. With the headless broomstick stretched out high in front of her and the base resting on her right shoulder she resembled a Prussian musketeer on the countermarch; her fellow soldiers crouched below her as she plunged the wooden bayonet into the on-switch of the wall-mounted television, and the attention of a few lucid patients advanced past her and into the screen. The nurse replaced the end of the stick into the broom head, about-turned and retreated to the door.

———

Hardy appeared at the police station wearing his striped pyjamas and a pair of old, untied brogues. His teardrops had formed a bib of wet cotton below his chin. Tall and narrow, with a full head of unruly grey-white hair and a long face that dripped to the floor, he looked unpredictable but controllable. At the request of the desk sergeant, he sat on an orange moulded plastic chair mounted on a pair of n-shaped, powder-coated metal tubes. Three seats away from him sat a younger man, perhaps in his forties, with a shaven head and a short beard, arms crossed over his torso, and fists that clenched the sides of a long, grey duffel coat. Leaning forward, he rocked slightly. But Hardy barely noticed him. Nor did he hear the low, muttered voices that leaked from the office behind the reception desk. His attention was on the swelling in his chest as his heavy heart pumped emptiness to his extremities. Cold air seeped through the aluminium-framed doors behind him.

'Keep it down, will ya? He'll hear you!'

'Doubt it. He's off his face. Hardly heard a word I said to him. He's on something, definitely.'

'Have you seen the age of him? Have a word with yourself. There's no way.'

'You go and take a look at him, then. He's in a right state.'

'Quiet! For Christ's sake, man.'

If Hardy had been looking, he would have seen a police officer lean his head out of the office and peer directly at him before darting back behind the wall.

'Probably got dementia or something. Probably

wandered out of a nursing home. Did you get his name?'

'Nah. Couldn't get it out of him. All I got was his wife's name. Reckons she gone missing.'

'Right, well that's a start. What's her name?'

'Mary.'

'Mary what?'

'That's all I got.'

'Oh, you're good. You should do this for a living.'

'That's what I'm saying. You need to speak to him. I can't get any sense.'

'Brilliant. Just what I need. Okay, I'll deal with it. But you need to go out there first and tell him to stop crying, right?'

———

Treetops had its own silence. In the days and weeks after Mary's departure, Hardy lay on various surfaces in the house and listened to the air while waiting for his thoughts to rest. The silence was different in every room and reflected the position of the contents within each one. An open drawer, a pair of crumpled trousers at the foot of the bed, discarded, used tissues on the arm of the sofa—every alteration changed the soundlessness in a unique way. By listening he could map the objects in the space around him; the position of the piano stool by the dresser; if the antique silver hand-mirror was facing up or down; which of her dresses he'd hung on the wardrobe door; whether or not he'd remembered to put the box of wedding photographs back into the cupboard under the television; how many unwashed plates lay next to the kitchen sink. With his eyes shut he could feel every inch of this house.

———————

Thirty years ago the space was everything he needed. An antidote to growing up in a back-to-back, sharing a bedroom with three brothers and, sometimes, a drunken father. The Hardy family filled Treetops with laughter and music. The children ran through the hallways and exploded into the expanse of lawn. Mary threw parties, hosted dinners and entertained his clients and their partners. Friends arrived unannounced and talked and danced into the early hours. That's what this house had been for. A space for living.

Hardy had not answered the telephone for some time and was unsure if his children would arrive for the monthly visit. Each of them, with spouse and an uncertain quantity of offspring, peered into the house from the front garden.

'Come on, dad. Open the door.'

One of the boys, his eldest he thought, spoke softly and slowly through the letterbox.

'I can see your reflection in the hallway mirror. Where's mum? Is she hiding down there with you? Dad? Dad, are you crying?'

———

The police search of Treetops did nothing to quell Hardy's tears. And now it wasn't just himself he cried for. He cried for his neighbours as they gathered at the end of their garden paths for a better view of the white incident tent that engulfed the house, and agreed in whispers about how there'd always been something odd about him. He cried for the passers-by who wondered where the crazy old man had hidden the body. And he cried for their children, for whose safety they worried. He cried for the couples who watched the report on the local evening news and, for the briefest of moments, regarded each other with suspicion. He cried for his own children, who wanted to believe the best but thought the worst. He cried for his and Mary's friends who could barely bring themselves to speak about what might have happened.

———

Continuous crying is not without health implications. If too much salt is lost, the level of fluid in the blood will drop. In severe cases, low sodium levels can lead to muscle cramps, nausea, vomiting, shock and, finally, death. According to Hardy's frustrated doctor, tears of sorrow have a higher salt content than those of joy or anger, compounding the problem further. The solution was 50mg salt capsules. Three a day was deemed ample.

Then there was the issue of internal drought. The doctor collected one hour's worth of tears from his patient. He calculated that Hardy needed to imbibe six extra pints of water per day to compensate. Consumption was to be increased on particularly wet days.

Salt water also matures the skin, and Hardy's now parchment-like face distressed his eldest son while he took his turn as the family representative at the monthly psychiatric assessment.

'I think that Mr Hardy is making good progress.'

Ms Crouch was a positive woman. Her detailed accounts of Hardy's minuscule steps towards recovery excited her. Little by little she was making this man better.

'Listening is a really, really important part of the therapeutic process. And your father is a very good listener.'

Hardy heard nothing. He cried for Ms Crouch's unconfident demeanour—the way she struggled to make eye contact with her clients' relatives and her colleagues. He cried for her attachment to her patients, for her disappointments.

'However, we need him to begin to contribute to the session.'

For her frailty, her self-consciousness and her confusion.

'For that to happen he will have to, well, start talking. But…'

He cried for his eldest son, who searched the face of a psychiatrist he had no confidence in for signs that this inconvenient insanity would end soon. For the boy's unasked questions and his anger.

'…I'm at a loss.'

———

'It is with regret, Mr Hardy, that I inform you we have decided to close your mother's case.'

The inspector's official tone was at odds with his body language, but Hardy's eldest had grown used to the man's disagreeable manner. Since failing to find a body or evidence to suggest that there might be one, Mrs Hardy's disappearance had become another unsolvable nuisance.

'When you say closed, what do you mean, exactly?'

'Well, we won't be looking for your mother any more.'

The tone switched to a slow enunciation.

'We've spent a lot of time and money searching for a woman who, if you want my personal opinion...'

'I don't. Thank you.'

'...has done a runner with her fancy feller and doesn't want to be bloody found.'

————

It was good to leave Treetops. The warmth and the gentleness of the other patients at St. Luke's cradled his broken heart. His new friends understood his emptiness, and they embraced him in a quilt of security and peace. And now the tears that stung his cheeks flowed from a quieter place.

Most of the staff preferred to keep their distance. Something about the tears disgusted them. When on duty, they would attend to him as quickly as possible, changing his wet clothing and bed sheets efficiently. The feelings he stirred made them uncomfortable and the desire to hurt him was sometimes too much to resist. However, there were some who tended Hardy that knew him as a gentle soul. They knew that his room was a sad place—that a longing for something out of reach charged the air, which affected them as they tended to him. For these few, the effect was of tranquillity—a calm acceptance. It forced them to consider their lot and to be content. And although it was never discussed, there was recognition among this small number that one always left Hardy's room in a calmer state of mind.

———

Hardy's eldest could see that his father's tears were thinning. He could see there was acquiescence in his heart. During the many afternoons they had spent together in the hospital games room and, weather permitting, in the grounds, he'd seen the old man's pain quieten. But he had also watched his body deteriorate, and now his father was so weak he could no longer feed himself.

'Dad, I've put the house on the market.' He stuttered as much reassurance into his voice as he could muster as he pushed Hardy's wheelchair into the television room. 'We need to pay for your care. It's not cheap, you know. And the money's got to come from somewhere.'

'Good afternoon, Mr Hardy.' A large smiling nurse boomed as she marched past the pair and out of the room, carrying a broom that rested on her shoulder.

Hardy's son parked the chair in front of the television.

'See you on Thursday, Dad.'

He kissed his father on the head and left.

————

The Inspector squinted at the muted television. A face on the screen was familiar. He swung his legs off the sofa and onto the ground so he could crouch forward for a better look. One of his bare feet knocked over a half-empty bottle of whisky, and the other landed on the remote control, which changed the programme to a documentary about the porn industry. He saved what he could from the bottle without diverting his eyes from the screen and settled back into the soft furnishings.

————

Hardy watched helplessly. A news report about another care home in another part of the country. Something about cuts. Something about losing staff. He stared past the smartly dressed presenter to where two patients were sitting, looking out into the air in front of them. Two women in dressing gowns. She was small and almost unseeable. Without looking at him, without saying a word, she was calling for him. The way she held her head and how her arms crossed at the wrists and rested on her lap. Her mouth hung open and her hair was shorter and greyer than he remembered. But she looked as beautiful as the day they'd met when she'd stared in wonderment as the fireworks exploded over their heads—the shadows hurrying over the sharp curves of her cheeks and jawbone, flashes of elegance and splendour, skin shining like a still lake. The report ended as tears clouded his vision—the liquid stung his neck and his towelling bib weighed heavy on his chest. They tasted different. Richer, perhaps.

THE STRAW HAT

I thought she was joking. But she stood there with the magazine article in one hand and a pen in another. Nothing in the waitress's face said more than the words she spoke, so I autographed the page and thanked her.

Later, I watched the traffic from my hotel window. Hundreds of cars and vans crawled along the street below, revving engines and blowing horns. Life down there seemed full of incident, of real drama and concern—people squeezing their way through London—workers struggling to find food and get to the office on time—women wheeling children to play-groups and nurseries—everyone just trying to stay on their feet as the hordes pushed past.

I saw an elderly man, in a white suit and straw hat, lean against a lamppost. An islet of stillness in the blur of the rapids. After a moment, he bent his head forward as he slipped his hand inside his jacket, and his hat fell off, landing upside down at his feet. He turned a little as if to look for the person who had knocked it off, or perhaps to ask for help. Then he bowed his head again. I imagined his eyes were shut as he willed his hat back. Then slowly, he slid down the metal post, with his arms wrapped around it, and lowered himself onto his knees. He reached towards the hat, but with his arm fully outstretched it was still a few inches away from him.

The crowd thickened, and a much younger man, talking on his mobile phone, tripped on the older man's arm. Without taking his hand away from his head or looking to see what had almost caused him to lose his footing, he recovered his balance and carried on walking. On all fours now, the man in the white suit extended an arm towards the hat again, only to watch it being kicked into the crowd and disappear under its hooves. He stayed where he was; his arm outstretched, and his head still turned towards the spot where the hat had been. A Royal Mail van lurched forward in the road and slowed again, breaking my line of sight, and as I waited for it to inch past my phone rang. Arthur was in the lobby. I picked up my coat and went downstairs.

We left the hotel and walked to the car. I looked to see if the man was still there. But everything seemed different at street level and I found it diffi-cult to work out my bearings. Arthur urged me to hurry, so I got into the car from where I continued to search.

'Hello? Have you gone deaf or something?'

His voice and the sudden lurch of the car into crawling traffic ripped me away from the window.

'What?'

'I said I've got some exciting news for you. Not that you're, like, interested or anything.'

'Sorry, it's just there was a man…'

'Right. I might have fucking guessed.'

'Oh, forget it. What were you saying?'

'So, you want to know now, do you?'

As I turned away from him, the warmth of my sigh met the cold of the window. The condensation looked like dry ice beneath the feet of the pedestrians.

'Look, I've told you about this before.' Tiny droplets of saliva landed on my arm as he spat his words through his tight mouth. 'Don't let all of this… all this new fame and stuff get to your little head. I've warned you about that.'

He had, and continued to do so every day. Having spent months doing everything he could do to 'big me up', to promise me people would love me, to put me 'in the zone', he now made it his business to ensure I didn't get 'carried away with it all'.

Our first meeting was in another large, busy hotel lobby, with several pillars and tall plants that separated a number of seating areas. I'd spotted him straight away, sitting on a sofa, holding a phone up to his cheek. He was already watching me when I saw him, but he looked away quickly as our eyes met. I knew it was him, and my heart dropped a little, as it continues to do every time we meet. He had the air of minor success about him, but it was incomplete. His head of over-abundant hair, the neatness of his clothes, the closeness of his shave and the confidence of his poise were good, but not enough. A work in progress. A temporary solution to a deep-rooted problem that had been becoming more apparent the better I got to know him.

'Now, are you listening? This is important.'

'What is?'

I continued to look out of the window at the torsos moving in our direction of travel, overtaking us as they weaved their way through one another. Other than the occasional splash of red, it was muted out there—dark blues, blacks, assorted greys and dull whites flowed and ebbed, blending together through the dirty car window. He spoke, but his tiresome voice mixed with the monotones outside—folding in on one another, swallowing each other up. No sooner did a navy blue skirt appear on the surface than it plunged into a wave of black overcoats and gunmetal scarves which, in turn, were overcome by a swell of colourless suits. Arthur kept talking as the car lurched forward a few metres and then slowed. The faceless tide of city colours washed past us again so it seemed like we were moving backwards. Again we rolled ahead, and again we slowed.

'We're about to go global. They can't get enough of you, sweetheart. This is big. D'you know what I'm saying?'

I looked back at him to see his mouth discharge a smile—tearing itself open over clenched, mother-of-pearl teeth. I'd never seen that row of marbleised cobblestones part. He spoke with them pressed together like an electromagnetic lock. His lips scraped over the irregular surface, forming the shapes needed to enunciate his puffery and preparations—to tell me something else was arranged—an interview with another magazine, a local television station appearance. I agreed to everything like I had a choice.

'How many people do you reckon watch that show? A-fucking-lot. That's how many. I'm telling you, this is it.'

I wondered if the man had found his hat, or if he was being trampled in the stampede. On his hands and knees, stretching his arm through the hard leather shoes and metal-tipped heels that cracked his bones and cut his flesh. With his bloodstained sleeves holding him off the ground, I imagined him pushing on, blind to pain and deaf to fear, straining for a glimpse of the straw hat.

I could get out of the car and find him. There is nothing to stop me. Just unfasten the seatbelt and go. Arthur's objections would fade and die somewhere behind me as I dived into the deadly currents. I am strong enough to hold my own, and I'd be able to fight my way through the shoulders and elbows as they tried to push me back. Every inch a battle— every step met with resistance and hostility.

In my mind, I throw myself in. My jaw clenched. Arms crossed tightly over my chest. And I thrust my way through until I catch sight of him. A flash of white. A bloodied face. Still anchored to the lamp post. I stretch for his hand until our fingertips meet, then we pull like we are clinging to the edge of a cliff —until the pads of our fingers find refuge in the folds of each other's knuckles. His warm skin is rough and dry—a large, steady hand that does not let me go as I turn my head in search of the straw hat. I see it right away, just out of range of my fully extended arm. I relax the muscles in my shoulders and soften the bones and elbow joints to gain extra length. He loosens his grip on the lamp post, and I get closer— so near that my fingertips imagine the texture of the brim. Then, without warning, we are cut loose from our mooring and set adrift under the legs and shoes, our bodies slamming against the concrete paving. I grab the hat and curl up to protect myself as we are dragged by the undercurrent. He pulls me closer and wraps his large form around me like a shell, and we close our eyes and wait to find out where the surge will take us. His broad back takes the knocks and the kicks as we hurtle through London for hours, unaware of our location of destination—holding our breaths and hoping for the best. Then we stop.

I open one eye and see we have been washed up between a red postbox and a red brick wall. The old man is already getting to his feet. The street is quiet and dark, and we are alone. He helps me up, I hand him the hat, and we laugh at how battered it is. Then, perhaps, we walk to a bar he knows, and I buy him a drink and we talk about his life and mine. He is widowed and lonely, suffering from an illness that affects his mobility. His only daughter lives in Toronto, and he doesn't want to worry her with his troubles. He used to dream of becoming a writer yet never wrote a word, but is content to wear this, alongside his other regrets, like a loose-fitting white suit. Then he listens to my story, and we agree there is no real sadness in all of this.

ARE YOU SCARED?

J: Me? No. What've I got to be scared about? Fads's the one who should be scared.

K: Just checking. Don't want you wimping out on me or anything.

J: You serious?

K: Nah. It's a joke. Just trying to lighten things up a bit.

J: A torch would've lightened things up, like.

K: Yeah, I know. Didn't think. But there's still some light. We've got a good hour yet before it gets proper dark. We'll be done before then.

J: I hope so.

K: Honestly, Jay, it's not far.

———

K: You know what this reminds me of? That time when we set all those trees on fire in the woods near your house.

J: We? Fads and me were just standing there. You lit the match.

K: It was mad though, wasn't it? Running down to your mam's house for buckets of water like we had a hope in hell of putting the fucker out.

J: They were sloshing around that much, do you remember? There was more water on our legs than in the buckets by the time we got back.

K: I'll never forget how quickly it spread, though.

J: I was shitting myself. It was well scary.

K: Aye, we all were. Remember how you said it was the Bowers lads who did it?

J: It was the first thing that came into my head. Thought we were going to go to prison or something.

K: You could've grassed me up.

J: Fuck off.

K: Have you ever told anyone the truth?

J: No.

K: Me neither.

———

K: Honestly, it's not far.

J: Do you think he knows we're coming?

K: He won't have a clue.

J: But he knows you know where he is?

K: Well, yeah. He asked me if he could use it when he called yesterday. I'm the only one who knows.

J: Not quite though, eh?

K: Well, as far as he's concerned.

J: Daft bastard.

K: Yeah.

———

J: Fuck me. Thought I just saw somebody in the trees over there. My eyes must be playing tricks on me.

K: Where?

J: Over there. It's nothing though. Just the trees.

K: Aye. It's getting darker. You've just got to stay focused.

J: It's a bit fucking difficult though. My feet are soaking.

K: Mine too.

————

K: You definitely brought the gun out of the car, didn't you?

J: Yeah.

K: Show me.

J: Here, look.

K: And you're sure you know how to use it?

J: Will you stop worrying! I've shot with me old man at the farm loads of times. You know that.

K: Yeah, but you use shotguns there.

J: For fuck's sake, Ken.

K: Sorry. I just want to make sure we get this right. We can't afford to fuck it up.

J: What's wrong with you? Look, I've got a gun you've got a gun. We'd have to be completely stupid to fuck it up. We just go in there, shoot the bastard and leave.

————

K: Remember how you and Fads used to wait for me to get off the school bus?

J: Ah, fuck. Not this again. Look, you were a scrawny little Scottish shit in a Catholic school blazer. What else were we supposed to do? Just let you walk home? Anyway, did you the world of good. Hardened you up.

K: Learned how to run fast as well. I used to shit myself when I saw you two at the bus stop. I had nightmares about it.

J: You were a total pussy. We taught you how to take a beating. We toughened you up. If you ask me, we did you a big favour.

K: Scarred me for life, more like.

J: Such a sensitive soul.

K: My mam used to give me a right bollocking when I got home. That blazer had more stitches than Barry Sheene. She was never bothered about the cuts all over my face though.

J: Probably couldn't see them through your tears, you soft twat.

————

J: They weren't trees though, were they?

K: What weren't?

J: You know, the fire. It wasn't trees you set light to.

K: Wasn't it?

J: No. They were gorse bushes. That's why the fire spread so quickly. Like tinder, those things.

K: Yeah, I think you're right.

J: Yeah.

———

K: Okay, so we need a plan.

J: Go on.

K: What I'm thinking is, when we get close to the caravan we split up and approach it from either side of the door. If you get there before me, you wait for me. I'll do the same if I get there first.

J: What about the back door?

K: It's a fucking caravan. There isn't a back door.

J: Well, I don't know do I? I've never been in a caravan before. So then what? We just open the door, go in and shoot him?

K: I reckon. The lock doesn't work. We're miles away from anywhere here and he'll be thinking he's pretty safe, so he won't have barricaded the door or anything. I'll do it if you want, though.

J: I reckon we both need to.

K: That might be a bit tricky, don't you think?

J: We could count down from three.

K: A countdown?

J: I just think it's important that we both do it. He fucked us both over. It's the principle.

K: Okay then. So a countdown from three? Do we shoot after one or on it?

J: Eh?

K: You know, is it three, two, one, shoot. Or three, two, shoot. Like on one instead of after it?

J: On one, I reckon.

K: And who counts down?

J: We should do it together.

———

K: It's funny to think how close us three used to be.

J: Yeah, I know.

K: And now we're going to do this.

J: He brought it on himself. He'd do the same to either one of us if we'd fucked him over like that.

K: That's what I'm saying though. One thing and that's it.

J: What do you mean?

K: Just that. All it takes is one thing. All those years we've been running together. All the shit we've been through. Fads fucks up and that's it, we kill him.

J: Hang on a minute. He scammed us.

K: Yeah, I suppose. Depending on how you look at it.

J: On how you look at it? I'm not getting this at all. This morning you were fucking raging. You said you were going to pull his arse out of his mouth. And now suddenly you're a fucking philosopher? Are you going soft in the head? We're supposed to be mates. He scammed us. You don't do that. And if you do, there's a fucking big price to pay. That's the unwritten rules.

K: Yeah, the rules. I know. You don't think it's harsh though?

J: No I don't. You've got to have rules. That's what keeps us all ticking along nicely. And if someone breaks them—then tough. We can't let this go. Once people find out that we let the fucker off for what he did, they'll think we're weak. And you know what'll happen then.

———

K: Laura's pregnant, you know?

J: What did you say?

K: I said Laura's pregnant.

J: Laura your sister?

K: Yeah.

J: She tell you that?

K: No. My mam did. She's really upset.

J: Your mam is?

K: Devastated. Laura's only just turned fourteen. You know what I'm saying? Fucking nightmare.

J: That's bad.

K: Tell me about it. When we've done with Fads that's next on my list.

J: How do you mean?

K: I'm going to kill the cunt who's been messing with her.

———

K: You know, when this is done it's just going to be you and me.

J: I was just thinking about that.

K: In what way?

J: What do you mean 'in what way'? As in electrical

fucking impulses jumping around my brain or whatever the fuck happens when you have a think about
something. What you on about?

K: I meant, what were you thinking? What are your
conclusions?

J: Conclusions? You a therapist as well as a philosopher now?

K: Cagey.

J: Fuck off.

K: Jesus Christ. Don't you think it's something we
need to talk about?

J: Why?

K: Well, only because of the tiny, almost insignificant
fact that it changes every-fucking-thing.

———

K: I'm not messing with you but are you sure you're
not scared?

J: Seriously, pack it in.

K: It's just you're very quiet.

J: I'm focusing, like you said.

———

J: You know what you were saying about your sister just then?

K: Yeah?

J: Do you know who it was?

K: She does.

J: She'll tell you?

K: No. But she's a shit liar. I'll work it out. Why? Do you know?

J: I've got a suspicion.

K: Who?

J: It's only a hunch.

K: Fucking who?

J: Fads.

K: What?

J: Like I say, it's only a hunch.

K: No way. Fads would never do that to me. What makes you say that?

J: Oh, so he'd steal your money but he wouldn't fuck your sister?

K: Are you telling me that you think Fads scamming us is worse than him fucking my underage sister?

J: I'm not saying that.

K: Then what are you saying? Because to me it sounds like you think my sister's just a piece of cheap meat.

J: Forget it.

K: Oh aye, I'm really going to let that one go. Go on, why do you think it was him?

J: It's just the way he looks at her, that's all.

K: What do you mean, the way he looks at her?

J: I don't know. It's a bit weird talking to you about it. It's just obvious that he fancies her.

K: For fuck's sake, Jay. She's fourteen.

J: I know, I'm just saying.

K: I need to get this straight in my head. What do you think is worse, stealing money or fucking a minor?

J: That one. The second one.

K: Let me hear you say it, which one is worse?

J: Fucking a kid is worse than stealing money.

K: Thank you.

———

J: We'll just carry on as we are.

K: What?

J: When it's just the two of us, we'll just carry on as we are.

K: Oh, right. Didn't know what you were talking about.

J: Except, I suppose we'll have to watch each other's backs a bit more because we'll be down a pair of eyes, won't we?

K: I suppose we will.

J: You know before, when I was thinking?

K: Yeah.

J: I was just thinking that it's funny, this shooting on one.

K: How do you mean?

J: Because there are three of us. Jay, Ken and Fads. People always say that, don't they?

K: I don't follow.

J: Jay, Ken, Fads. Three, two, one.

K: Still not following.

J: You know, Jay, Ken, Fads. Three, two, one. We shoot on one. It's like we shoot the one. Get what I'm saying?

K: Getting a bit deep for me there, Jay. And I thought I was supposed to be the philosopher.

————

K: There it is.

J: Where?

K: Just up there. Look. Behind those bushes. See the roof?

J: I can't see anything, it's too dark. Oh, hang on. I see it.

K: He's probably sleeping. Are you ready?

————

J: Shit. Where are the lights?

K: I'll get them. Hang on. There.

J: It doesn't look like anyone's been staying here. Are you sure this is the right place?

K: I'm very sure.

J: Where is he then?

K: You could try looking behind you.

J: What?

F: Surprise.

J: What the fuck?

F: Put the gun down, Jay.

J: You've got this all wrong, Fads.

F: I don't think so.

J: Tell him, Ken. You put your gun down and we'll put ours down.

F: Put the fucking gun down, Jay.

K: It doesn't matter if he puts it down or not. It's not loaded.

J: What? What the fuck is going on?

K: Unwritten rules, Jay. That's what's going on.

J: Why you pointing that at me? I don't understand. What rules?

K: What rules? Let's start with the one that says you don't fuck my sister?

J: I don't know what you're talking about, Ken. Honestly.

K: How about the rule that says you especially don't fuck my sister when she doesn't want you to fuck her.

J: Is this some kind of joke?

F: Fucking hilarious, isn't it.

K: It's dead simple really. Fads didn't fuck us over. We made that up to get you here. What happened is that you raped my sister and now she's pregnant.

J: Okay, okay, look, we had a thing for a little while, me and Laura, but I didn't rape her for fuck's sake!

K: She's fourteen.

J: Yeah, but she doesn't look it, does she?

K: Seriously? That's your defence? You fucking peado.

J: Come on, Fads, what I have ever done to you?

F: Nothing. Well, apart from the fact you were happy to blow my brains out a minute ago.

J: No, that was Ken's idea. I didn't...

F: Ready Ken? On one?

A SURVIVAL GUIDE FOR THE UNSEEN

Paris, 17th September 1894.

You will have questions. That is understandable. I have done all I can to anticipate and answer as many as possible. At this very moment, it is unlikely that you will grasp the value of the work I have put into these pages. In time, however, when you begin to realise that the information herein will help you comprehend and escape from your difficulties, I believe you come to be thankful for the efforts I have made. That said, gratitude is not what I seek. Sharing this document with you is the least I could do.

When I was rendered unseen my predecessor neglected to offer me any assistance, which resulted in many years of confusion. I daresay he received little or no help when he was struck invisible and saw no reason to come to my aid. That is not the way I approach life. You have taken an enormous burden from me, and I owe you an explanation. But first, let us address your questions by dealing with the one that should be at the top of your list: with whom does the responsibility of your invisibility belong? Or, who has done this to you? I have already answered: I am to blame. At this juncture I am tempted to offer my excuses and apologise for committing such a dreadful crime, but there will be time for that later.

Now let us begin. For the purpose of this guide, it is useful to remember your life as it was in the weeks running up to the present. You will have perceived a change in the number of people who looked at you while you were in public. It may have felt as if you were more familiar or recognisable than you used to be. You noticed a significant increase, did you not? This was due to the strength of your 'colour', which I began enlarging some time ago.

The stronger and larger your colour, the more magnetic your presence. On the other hand, a weak, dull colour can fail to attract attention at all. Often, the only way an individual with a flaccid colour can persuade another to see him is by placing himself into their immediate field of vision. However, even this is no guarantee. Yours reached a stage when people could not help but notice you. It may have seemed as if an invisible force was physically turning heads towards you. I call these colours 'visual scent'. I have named them this as they appear to possess olfactory characteristics as well as visual. Of course, in the visible world one can neither see nor smell these colours, but I believe the name helps in our understanding of the phenomenon.

We are unaware of visual scents before becoming unseen, and are confronted by them for the first time immediately upon losing visibility, as you undoubtedly were. Therefore, it seemed reasonable to assume that these colours have something to do with the predicament, and that is why I decided to dedicate my time to the study of them.

The first thing I noted in addition to colour variation was that visual scents differ in the amount of space they occupy around a person. It was these dimensions that interested me the most. So, if you will indulge me, I would now like to present you with my hypothesis. From the observations I made in the years after becoming unseen, I came to believe that when my visibility was stolen something else was also taken. In fact, I am convinced visibility itself is merely a side effect of that which was taken from me. The 'something else' to which I refer is visual scent. (It will not have escaped your attention whilst reading this that you do not appear to possess one.) I propose that it is possible to control the size of the visual scent of another living being and, in doing so, alter their visibility.

My initial investigations considered this question: why do the visual scents of certain individuals have greater power than others? I began seeking answers by roaming the streets to find people with powerful scents. Upon identifying the subjects, I would follow them and learn what I could about their lives. In total, I singled out twenty-three persons with significantly enlarged visual scents. Out of these subjects, sixteen of them were suffering from a severe amount of distress, and the remainder appeared to enjoy a certain amount of fame. Naturally, I called these groups the Distressed and the Renowned.

The first group, the Distressed, experienced relatively short periods of enlarged visual scent. Indeed, it lasted only for as long as the distress itself. The cause of the suffering varied considerably, ranging from the death or loss in some other way of a loved one, to tremendous dread or worry; being in fear for one's own life, for instance. The colours these people tended to exude fluctuated, but all of them were extremely dark.

Unlike the first group, for whom the source of enlargement was usually easy to identify, I often found it difficult to ascertain the origins of the second group's expansion. It was intriguing, however, that while their scents varied in volume, the colour was always the same (a hideously vivid blue). It was a blue that I had never seen before; a colour so intense it hurt my eyes to look at it for more than a few seconds at a time. What is more, the Renowned (which included well-known actors, politicians and artists) experienced much longer periods of enlargement, which I assume continued until their renown eventually waned, although I did not experience this decline with my own eyes. So, my conclusion from this investigation is that heightened levels of distress and fame result in enlarged visual scents and increased visibility, and that the second grouping enjoys greater longevity and uniformity of colour.

My second investigation was to establish if it is possible to control a person's visibility by manipulating his visual scent. I developed two strategies: one to create a heightened level of distress and the other to generate sufficient fame. I selected two subjects, both males in their mid-twenties. I will call them Subject A and Subject B. Both appeared to be mentally stable and leading what I can only describe as 'average' lives.

Subject A worked as a butcher in a meat market. He had a wife and one young child. His network of associates seemed to be restricted to colleagues, some customers and extended family. Deciding on the appropriate way to raise the subject's distress to an adequate level proved particularly challenging.

Although I appreciate this has little to do with the experiment, I am not a scientist and I found I was, at first, unable to remove myself emotionally from my investigations. It was essential my endeavours did not adversely affect the lives and states of mind of my subjects in the long term. Therefore, I chose an action that, while causing immediate distress, could be remedied as soon as I had the evidence I required.

After watching Subject A for some time, I learned some of his more regular habits and was able to predict certain routines with some accuracy. I knew he and his young family visited his wife's mother in Montreuil every Sunday afternoon. I also knew that, approximately two hours after their arrival, the child would become hysterical and Subject A would leave the property with it in a perambulator. Each week he would push the contraption along Rue de la Solidarité and Rue des Quatre Ruelles until they reached Parc des Beaumonts. Once there, he circumnavigated the park until the child fell asleep, and then returned to the house via the same route in reverse.

On the day of the experiment, he and the child arrived on schedule. The park, as it always seemed to be, was busy. Middle-class couples held each other's hands, or those of their children, and paraded slowly through the grounds. The weather (quite grey and damp) had not put them off. Although I had no reason to hide, I stood by a large ash tree until Subject A had passed. Then I followed him at a respectable distance until I was ready to act. The subject stopped, as he always did at this point, to light a small cigar. I came parallel with the perambulator and, as the subject brought a lighted match to his face, I reached in and removed the now sleeping child, covered it with my coat and returned to my position behind Subject A. There was no need hide the infant as anything I have on my person, from clothes to objects, also become unseeable. However it seemed prudent to protect the child from the elements so that it didn't wake up. When Subject A resumed his progress I fell in behind him once again.

Several minutes passed before there was a reaction, which gave me time to observe his visual scent. It was its usual light emerald colour that emanated no more than two feet from his centre, which is only a little above average. His slow pace, the way he casually lifted his face to the sky as he exhaled the smoke, and his sly glances at passing ladies all confirmed he had not yet noticed the infant's absence. He paused once again, this time to extinguish the cigar butt on the ground with his foot, and took three more steps before stopping once more. From where I stood, I saw him bend at the waist and bring his face closer to the perambulator. He called the child's name and reached into the apparatus, pulling out a small, embroidered blanket, which he let fall to his feet. His back straightened, and I assumed this was when the reality of the situation reached the appropriate part of the brain as his visual scent changed abruptly. As it grew in volume, it darkened to a thick hazelnut brown so dense that I struggled to see the subject within it. I also observed that immediately before he had the opportunity to speak or draw attention to himself, a number of other walkers turned their gaze towards him; some of them stopping in their tracks as they did so.

Within seconds, Subject A was looking about him and speaking to these people in a raised voice. He walked away from the perambulator and then back to it several times, and scanned the park in a decidedly erratic fashion. All the while the sphere grew larger. More people moved towards him until a small crowd surrounded him, one or two members of which were asking him questions. Suddenly, he broke away from the group to survey the park without obstruction, as if he hoped to spot the minor laying upon the path he had just traversed. At this point, I walked into the gathering, returned the child to the carriage, and stood back to observe the outcome.

The reappearance was soon noted and the subject was alerted. He dashed back to the perambulator and scooped the child into his arms. Immediately, his sphere began to lessen in density and size at about a quarter of the speed at which it had expanded. The crowd started to disperse and the subject, who had been cradling his child for two or three minutes, placed it back into its lying position and marched back to his mother-in-law's house. His visual scent did not return to its original proportions or colour before he reached the front door, but it was by now a fraction of the size it had been in the park.

Later, while pondering the results of this experiment, I recalled that while I existed in the visible world, sometimes, as I walked through busy parts of the city where scores of people might have surrounded me, my attention would occasionally be drawn to an individual who was weeping, or visibly upset in some other way. I would have thought little of it at the time, reasoning that the unusual public display of emotion was in itself enough to attract my eye. On reflection, however, I believe these troubled creatures were often outside of my focal plane and that I had actually turned my head to see them. This meant that something else must have made me mindful of their distress. From the evidence I had gathered on the day of the experiment, I concluded that this effect must be a direct consequence of the expanded magnetism of their visual scents.

Subject B was a hotel porter at L'Hôtel Gramont. He lived at the hotel, in staff quarters, was unmarried and, as far as I could tell, had no contact with any immediate family. Also, he had an extensive social circle, which mainly comprised of other hotel employees. Most of his spare time and money was spent in the bistros with his co-workers.

As in the experiment with Subject A, I asserted a strict moral code: whatever level of fame I achieved for Subject B, I had to ensure that it benefited his life in addition to furthering my understanding. This meant making sure it brought him the kind of attention that would be of use to him.

I spent many weeks studying Subject B. He seemed to be proficient at his job. He was strong and energetic; his language and manner were efficient with staff, and he was gracious and polite to guests; and he had that particular skill all good porters possess: the ability to virtually disappear when standing at the front of the hotel so the head porter becomes as prominent as a grand statue. He was also an excellent drinker. The young waiters, apprentice chefs, kitchen hands and other hotel workers with whom he spent most of his leisure time were monstrous in their appetite for wine. Late at night they would descend upon their favourite cheap restaurants, eat quickly and drink ferociously. It was quite common for them to wake in the morning at the same table where they drank the night before, and to not so much as lay their eyes, never mind their bodies, upon their beds for days on end. How they managed to follow this behaviour with a day of relentless labour, I never was able to fathom. This was the life they led. However, while Subject B embraced this existence in many ways, he was also the exception to the rule. Although he attended the bistros and drank heartily, he was more careful than the others and moderated his consumption by returning to his quarters at the same time every night to ensure he was neat, shaven and at his post punctually every morning. He was able to behave like this without attracting much resistance or suspicion from his peers because his visual scent was weak and his presence was rarely felt or missed.

While I sensed a modest amount of ambition in the young man, which would, I reasoned, make the experiment easier, he did not appear to be in possession of any talent to speak of; his physical appearance was decidedly unimpressive, and his intelligence was nothing to boast about. After much deliberation, I decided that *I* must become the special ability that would bring him fame.

Whenever the subject had a day's leave from his duties, which was an extremely rare occurrence, he would walk alone to Boulevard Haussmann where he peered into shop windows and admired expensive gentlemen's attire. On one visit, he eyed a particularly luxurious necktie that was on display at the establishment of a well-known Austrian tailor. As he stared, I entered the premises, located the tie in the window and waited for Subject B's gaze to stray. Sure enough it did, and I picked up the tie and exited. I then placed the item in the subject's coat pocket. I didn't have long to wait for a reaction. As he moved away from the shop he put his hands into his pockets, as he was in the habit of doing while walking, and immediately pulled out the tie. He looked at it, then back at the shop so many times over the next few seconds that I lost count. Then he placed the tie back into his pocket, returned to the shop front, dropped the item on the ground and walked back to L'Hôtel Gramont with considerable haste.

Keen to build some momentum, the next day I initiated my campaign in earnest. I began by bringing Subject B objects that he looked at for any length of time. My first delivery that morning was his shoes. As he sat on the edge of his bed fastening his shirt, he glanced over at his brown boots, which were by the door to his chamber. The moment his eyes returned to his shirt buttons, I placed the shoes by his feet. At first, he seemed unperturbed and began to put them on. Then he paused, looked over to where the shoes had been, and back at his feet. He remained in that position, one finger on the inside right heel, foot half inserted, while his eyes seemed to scan the room for clues as to what had just happened.

He ate breakfast with other hotel workers on a long, rough wooden table in a room adjacent to the kitchen area. I made sure the salt was with him before he'd had the opportunity to ask for it to be passed down the table. Later, when he stared at the female kitchen hand who had made a point of ignoring him every morning of my observations thus far, I placed my hands on the sides of her face and gently turned her gaze to his, and they smiled at one another.

As he stood to attention outside on the steps of the hotel, I moved the luggage that had been dumped from the carriages to his feet before he had been permitted to move by the head porter. When a female guest dropped her umbrella, I ensured it was in his hand before anyone else had a chance to retrieve it for her. And so it went.

By sundown, the subject was experimenting with his new-found skill. On the way to that evening's bistro, he stopped and threw his hat to the ground. Seconds later it was back on his head. He moved a tray of apples from one corner of a fruit seller's stall to the other by merely staring at it. He plucked a single rose from a florist's lavish display and planted it into the hair of a young lady who was strolling with a friend on the other side of the road. After a while, he found that although the results of his ability were often unpredictable they always pleased him. However, for the sake of pragmatism and to avoid my own physical exhaustion, it was important he realised that there were limits to his powers. This meant disappointing him every now and again. When I saw him staring hard at a stationary carriage, I tugged gently horse's reins which did little more than to force it to move its head. And when it looked to me as if he was attempting to ignite a streetlight, I did nothing.

He entered the bistro unnoticed as usual, and ate and drank his normal quantities without attempting anything out of the ordinary. But when the hour arrived at which he would usually leave, he ordered another cup of wine instead. He listened to the others talk and laughed when a joke was shared. At a little after midnight, he watched as two men attempted to amuse the restaurant owner's daughter. She regarded them with half-interest as they hid a coin under one upturned cup and then slid it around the tabletop with two others.

'Look closer this time,' one of them suggested when the owner's daughter failed to guess which cup the coin was under. After the fifth attempt, the girl yawned and turned away. Then Subject B spoke for the first time.

'Watch this.'

He stared at the upturned cups on the men's table. I moved swiftly to retrieve the cup with the coin under it and place it on the subject's table. For the men, and the daughter who had glanced over her shoulder on hearing the new voice, the cup disappeared and then reappeared in front of the young man, who they had barely been aware of up until that point. Their surprise was undoubtedly tinged with fear, and when Subject B lifted the cup to reveal the coin, one of the men stood up, knocking his chair to the ground, and the daughter dropped her glass to the floor.

The following night, and each night for the next two weeks, Subject B performed to a full house at the bistro, and his visual scent steadily swelled. For every 'show' we did something different, from swapping people's hats to making their tables float inches from the ground, and the crowd gasped in wonder. Word of these wonders spread, and it was not long until, one evening, a gentleman in a grey top hat invited him to appear at Le Chat Noir in Montmartre. He accepted and dutifully silenced a notoriously rowdy and diffi-cult-to-please audience. His act became a nightly feature, and his hotel position a thing of the past. With every performance, Subject B's visual scent grew in volume and became unbearably blue. In fact, there were times on stage when I found it excruci-ating to look at him; and the more he performed the greater its severity became.

The way in which Subject B's scent grew was quite different from the growth of Subject A's. This led to a better understanding as to how visual scent is gener-ated. When in distress, the body appears to produce its own, which I suspect is some kind of self-preser-vation mechanism that has evolved to attract the help of others during times of great need. For the Renowned, however, it is quite different. Having turned blue, this type grows by plundering the scents of others. While he was on stage, and later when walking along busy streets, I witnessed hundreds of slithers or pulses of colour being sucked from the scents of others and plunging into Subject B's, causing it to expand continuously.

Satisfied that I had proved my theory, I commenced my exit strategy. Obviously, this arrangement could not last without my sustained contribution, and I had no intention of carrying on indefinitely. At the same time, I had no wish to cut off his powers without warning; after all, the subject had gone through significant life changes for my benefit. I started my retreat by reducing the number of times I responded to his demands during rehearsals. Over the course of a month, I cut the number down from as many as I could physically react to, to one in every five requests. Eventually he did as I had hoped – he consulted a magician performer whom he had befriended. The magician sold him a number of tricks that he could perform in addition to his own. Subject B introduced these new elements into his act slowly, and while I was loyal to him on stage, I gave him all the encouragement he needed to diversify by occasionally remaining uncooperative between performances. By the time I withdrew entirely, Subject B had a new act and a promising career ahead of him.

I had proven to my satisfaction that my hypothesis was true – that it is indeed possible to control the visual scent of another and alter their visibility in the process; and that visibility is in itself little more than a by-product of visual scent, albeit a very useful one. It then seemed to me that the next step in my investigations would be to demonstrate beyond all doubt (or, at least, to satisfy my relatively undemanding requirements of proof) that my invisibility was a direct symptom of there being no visual scent around my person. However, I struggled with this. I consider myself to be a resourceful man of reasonable inventiveness, to be in possession of a creative mind and above average intelligence. Despite all of this, I confess, I could not find a way to remove the visual scent of a subject and prove this second theory. All I had was my own story and the clues I found within it.

I believe my visual scent was taken from me by a Mister Lupin, a gentleman who I thought was giving me everything I had ever dreamed of but, in reality, was stealing it. The man was a thief with a motive with which I can now fully empathise.

Before I became unseen, I was a publisher who enjoyed modest success. I published four journals each month, two scientific, one about European architecture, and one on the literature of the day. The latter was my passion, although I did not contribute to it in any way other than its publication.

Some time ago, I became aware of a manifestation in my home. In the beginning, it was only apparent in the library, a room which, apart from the occasional visit by a member of my staff, was used only by me. I recall the very first time I became conscious of a presence: I was sitting comfortably in my favourite armchair reading about the life of the publisher Henri Estienne, in whom I was particularly interested at that time. I distinctly remember feeling quite untroubled by the fact that, in the corner of my eye, I could see somebody sitting on the chair (a rather disagreeable thing in dire need of reupholstering which I had considered disposing of many times) in the corner of the room. As I read, I mentally acknowledged and accepted the extra person in the library as if their being there was perfectly reasonable. This remained the case for some seconds until my rational brain caught up with the rest of my mind, which was when I remembered that there had not been another person in the library when I crossed the threshold, and I had not permitted anyone to enter since. Of course, when I turned to look in the direction of the intruder there was nothing to see except for an empty chair. This occurred on numerous occasions and, while I was often confused by it, I never felt fear. There was something natural and, if I dare say, ordinary about these visits. I never mentioned it to my wife for I knew she would think the house haunted and insist on moving to another. Time progressed and eventually I became so accustomed to the presence in my library I didn't give it a second thought.

What I find most disconcerting about this period is that when I try to remember the timescales involved,

I draw a blank. I have no idea for how long I shared my library with this other being. It really could have been anything from weeks to years. What I do remember, however, is the first time we communicated. I was reading an article on behalf of the editor of *La Connaissance*, one of the journals I published, as he had been struck ill. The writer of the piece had taken it upon himself to make each sentence as impenetrable as humanly possible and reading his text was quite excruciating. Each time I finished a paragraph with a modicum of understanding of what the gentleman might be trying to say, I had to rest. It was during one of these moments of mental recuperation that I became aware, as was quite normal by this time, of the apparition on the outer limits of my vision. I am not sure why I decided at this time over others to speak to it, but speak to it I did.

'Are you real?' I asked.

And to my astonishment, he (for this was the first time I became aware of its gender) replied, 'Yes'!

The very moment he spoke, I lost sight of him and did not regain it for several days. At first, I thought I had scared him away. However, I later discovered that he had been there all along and that I had simply been looking too hard; the act of searching made it impossible for me to see him because, as I now know, the unseen exist on the periphery.

Our verbal communication did not develop further

than this as I found it impossible to not direct my attention towards him as I spoke, which was the very act that rendered him invisible. So we began writing to each other instead. First, I asked him who he was. He told me his name was Lupin and that he was my imagination personified. He went on to explain that somehow I had unlocked a part of my creative brain that very few people manage to access, and that the only explanation for this phenomenon was that I must be a genius. Then, he told me that having the ability to converse with one's imagination was a great gift and that I should make full use of him for my advantage. Finally, he added that to doubt my imagination would likely weaken and eventually destroy this new power. I am fully aware of how foolish and gullible I must seem. However, put yourself in my position: suspension of disbelief had been the standard ever since a mysterious entity began appearing to me in my home. If he had told me I was the Emperor of France and my life up until that point had been a dream, I dare say I would have regarded it as the truth.

From that point, our dialogues took the form of a series of questions from him and my dutiful answers. Without me realising at the time, his queries became steadily more intimate until I was revealing some of my deepest secrets, several of which I had never shared with a soul before. There was something calming and confessional about these exchanges, and

I was strangely at ease while divulging the full cata-
logue of my frustrations, weaknesses and aspira-
tions. It was not long before told him about how I
yearned to be a famous novelist and be respected for
my own writing rather than for being a mere facili-
tator for other writers, an ambition I hadn't even
dared reveal to my wife. We wrote to one another on
this subject for a few days before he told me to start
writing.

Lupin fed me the most incredible stories. All I had to
do was type up what he wrote down. They were
wonderfully crafted works that gave life to the most
heart-wrenchingly vulnerable, impossibly heroic,
beautiful and repulsive characters the likes of which I
had never dreamed of creating. I typed like a man
possessed, terrified that my newly discovered imagination would wither and die before I completed the
next chapter. As soon as I had finished the first novel,
I published it using my own resources. Each print run
sold out within weeks, and every month for six
months I called for my men to deliver a new creation
to the booksellers of Paris. The quality and quantity
of the works astonished the city and I was hailed as a
genius, confirming Lupin's assertion.

The income from this venture was more rewarding
than anything I had ever aspired to, and the fame was
quite overwhelming. Everywhere I went I was
approached by strangers who asked to shake my hand
and enquired after my secret, which I gave willingly

and with more than an ounce of pride: I have a very active imagination, I would reply.

I was invited to parties every night of the week, most of which I would attend in order to bask in others' appreciation of my brilliance. The attention was like nectar for my heart and I could not satisfy its thirst. Lupin worked tirelessly for his novelist master, and when he gave me the idea to send my works for translation abroad, to London and Madrid, I acted on it immediately. While I prepared my work for transportation, I dreamt of becoming the most famous living author in Europe. The money no longer mattered as my craving for celebrity now drove me. And as I waited for the response from foreign cities, I boasted to my many friends about my upward trajectory and was invigorated by their widened eyes and gaping mouths. I insisted the editor of my literary journal commissioned articles on my endeavours, and soon the whole of Paris knew that I was preparing for the international renown that was set to follow.

Madrid was the first to answer, although its reply arrived by an unexpected means: via the front page of *L'Écho* de Paris. It was something of a shock to read I was being accused of plagiarism by the very publisher to whom I had sent my work. He, the newspaper declared in a rather impertinent manner, represented the estate of Armando Baus, whose work I was supposed to have passed off as my own. Indeed the evidence certainly suggested that I was guilty of this crime. The newspaper compared several passages of my work to Baus's, demonstrating that they were, apart from a few words here and there, identical. The newspaper went on to proclaim me a fraud and challenged me to defend myself. Of course, I penned a response right away. With the help of Lupin, I demanded a public apology and full retraction of the accusation. I argued that any fool could copy my work and present a few examples to a gullible newspaper. I demanded to know how much money the journalist had paid for this slanderous information.

The letter was printed in the next edition, along with further evidence of my alleged theft. My indignation was apt for a man of my fame and stature and, encouraged by Lupin, I determined that I would not allow this character assassination attempt to come between me and my public, and I would attend the party of a well-known heiress that very evening as I had nothing to hide.

On arrival, I sensed I was receiving greater attention than on previous occasions, yet every look with which I engaged was broken quickly and embarrassedly. Not one person dared to hold my gaze. The reception I had become accustomed to did not appear, and every attempt I made to join or begin conversation was shunned, yet when I turned my back I could feel their judgemental eyes upon me. I marched my anger to the main foyer of the house, where two hundred or so guests ceased talking, one by one. I climbed six steps of the large stairway and, as I turned to address the silenced crowd, I noticed that Lupin was by my side. With added confidence to fuel my indignation, I told the throng they were fools to believe the lies that had been printed about me; that every word I had ever written was from my own imagination; that they had been privileged to have had the opportunity to share in my wondrous literary inventions; and they had no right to behave towards me with anything less than the highest respect.

As I spoke, I felt my imagination wrap his arms around my torso, propping me up, giving me the physical support and help I needed to get through this challenging time. I remember thinking I must have looked weak on my feet, and I was thankful for a servant like Lupin. As the pressure increased on my ribcage, I noticed the people below seemed to change in two ways: they had become encapsulated in the most wonderful colours, translucent like the first strokes of watercolour over pencil marks on a crisp white canvas; and they had stopped listening to me. Instead, they were whispering to each other, some with hands over gaping mouths, and pointing at the stairs towards the man standing next to me. When I turned to see who dared to divert my audience's attention, I saw Lupin. Through a vivid blue filter, I could see that his beard was trimmed, his hair was groomed and he wore my clothes. As he skipped down the stairs and into the ocean of colour below, I realised I was focusing directly on him for the first time.

I remained on the stairs for a while longer, holding tightly to the bannister and bellowing at the rainbow hordes, commanding them to listen to what I had to say, but they continued to ignore me. I descended and screamed in their faces, but they heard nothing. I knocked their drinks to the floor and pushed them and, while they stumbled and staggered to retain their footing, they still did not see me. I fell at their feet and wept, and they walked around me.

When I returned home, I found that my safe, in which I kept the money I made from my writing, was empty. When my wife returned, she could not see or hear me either. I sat in my library for days and here I have to end my story as I plunged into a despair so deep I remember nothing of it. All I know is that one day I emerged.

Lupin went to considerable effort to devise and execute a plan that would free him from the unseen. Having found me to be a suitable candidate, he helped me achieve a dream that I had buried many years before, and once it was realised he was able to steal my visibility.

My visual scent must have reached a spectacular size, for I was very well known throughout Paris and much of the French-speaking world. I was ripe for the picking. He was an empty vessel and the act of wrapping himself around me was all he needed to do to drain my visual scent and claim it as his own.

Could I do the same to another? Could I plunge a fellow human being into such an abyss? Indeed, it would have been a simple matter to take the visual scent of Subject B. And you are perfectly entitled to ask why I did not; why choose to rob you when I had ample opportunity to free myself at the expense of someone else. My answer is I could not bring myself to betray a young man who had helped me so much with my learning. That is no consolation to you, I know. Perhaps had I set out with the intention of stealing from him I would have been able to go through with such a terrible deed.

In my defence, I spent many years trying to find an alternative method. My most promising effort came when I discovered that, in addition to the Distressed and the Renowned, there is an interesting third category. I have mentioned already that being in fear for one's life had the effect of generating a sizeable visual scent. I discovered this because of an incident I witnessed on Boulevard de Courcelles. While on an afternoon stroll, I became aware of a presence in the street. I knew it was moving quickly even before I laid eyes on the source. A young man, certainly no more than twenty years of age, was running so fast it was as if Satan himself were on his heels. His pursuers were a group of three men, approximately ten years his senior. The young man fell to the ground within twenty or so yards of me and, in the few seconds it took the men to reach him, I could do nothing but admire the size of his dark grey sphere. It engulfed a good fifty people around him and I, for one, felt his fear scrape down my spine. The passersby in close proximity to the men shifted chaotically and it was difficult for me to see what exactly happened, but I could hear shouting and see flickers of a struggle, and I knew the men were upon him. After a scream, the young man was fleeing again through the crowd, but this time he was not pursued. I pushed through the onlookers and saw that one of the pursuers lay bleeding in the road. Another knelt next to him and held his head, while the third stood by, shuffling his feet nervously. By now, the injured man was surrounded in a dark blue and brown swell. A moment passed and the kneeling man looked up at his companion and shook his head. The standing man said something with quiet urgency and then tugged at the other's coat until he got to his feet. Then they walked away in haste, leaving the injured man behind.

For those of us who stayed to watch, there was a definite moment at which life left the wretched lump. The air became thicker and warmer, which is something I am sure those around me also noticed, and there were gasps and the covering of mouths.

However, my affiliation with the crowd ended there as I was the only one who seemed aware of the eruption of colour that burst from the corpse less than a second later. At first, I thought it was one colour, but, if it was, it quickly split into many, far greater in number and magnitude than any rainbow. The shock of the explosion knocked me from my feet and, as I watched, the colours reached twenty or more yards into the sky and in every direction. The force soon lessened and the tentacles of colour froze in the air for a moment before falling to the ground like felled trees. Where there had been blood, now rivers of every pigment pulsed from the body as if pumped from the corpse's heart. They flowed, retaining their own identities until they merged under the feet of the carcass-watchers, blending to form a filthy, dark swamp, the hue of which I had never seen before and find utterly impossible to describe.

Something else erupted from the corpse on that day: a new theory that, if it worked, would give me the power to end this curse once and for all, and liberate myself from an appalling guilt that was already bearing heavily on me like a boot upon a garden pea. I would attempt to take the visual scent from a freshly deceased body.

The excitement gripped me so tightly I could barely breathe, and I wasted no time getting to Hôtel-Dieu, the nearest hospital. I inspected the beds until I had identified a cluster of poor souls who looked as if they were hanging on to life by the thin, brittle grey hairs on their wizened heads. I pulled a chair into the middle of the ward and began my vigil.

Eight deathbeds surrounded me, the occupant of each one a potential door back to the world I longed to be a part of once more. Nurses, doctors and visitors poured in and out of the room, and it didn't take long before I was able to narrow my search. A large, middle-aged man, enclosed in a dirty orange cloud, stood at the foot of a bed at the far end of the ward. A doctor spoke to him in grave tones and the man brought his hands to his face. The elderly woman in the bed appeared to be unconscious and oblivious to their conversation. The doctor left and the man rested his substantial weight on the bottom corner of the woman's bed and whispered to her in a language I did not know. I moved my chair nearer to the pair and waited.

Night fell and the man struggled to stay awake. I saw him nip his leg with a thumb and forefinger, each digit as thick as a baby's wrist. Sleep eventually took him and I was left alone with the woman. I stood over her and listened to her breathing in the fading lamplight. Each inhalation was infinitesimally shorter and shallower than the one before it. Her silhouette sank into the bed as I studied her carefully and bided my time. Her lung capacity continued to diminish, and her breath grew weaker still. And then she began to slip. I climbed onto the bed and held her.

Vibrations in the air quickly compensated for the old woman's stillness. At first, it was like being bombarded with thousands of tiny, invisible bubbles that tapped at the skin of my face and hands with a relentless and torturous intensity. I slid one arm under her neck and the other over her chest and clasped my fingers together noticing that, in my embrace, she felt much thinner than she had looked. Then she erupted. There was no beginning; the colours just appeared. Violent jets of blues and greens and yellows tore through the ward like ferocious rainbow demons determined to rip the world apart. Terrified, I held on as tightly as I could to stop being blown from the bed, as if this thin corpse was the anchor that would save me. I closed my eyes, opened my mouth as wide as I could, and breathed as deeply as my lungs would let me. Again and again I drank in the visual scent until the darkness behind my eyelids spread to my consciousness.

I have memories of slipping in and out of oblivion. I remember the room appearing to shake, screams that may have been my own, crying emanating from the darkness, and being as cold as the stone floor on which I laid. Sounds were slow and deep, and everything was black even though light burnt through the windows. I may have been there for days.

When I was eventually able to pull myself to my feet, I was still in the ward: eight new occupants, one dead already and others well on their way. Outside, I could feel the sun against my skin but there was no warmth, and I trembled and stumbled my way through streets of caustic air. Sometime later I woke up under the arches of Pont Marie, still wearing the clothes that I had been soiling for days. For the next weeks, I was plagued by double vision and nausea of unearthly severity. Never again did it cross my mind to remove the visual scent of a corpse, and nor should it yours.

Alas, I identified you as my ideal donor and applied all this understanding so as to win my freedom. I increased the dimensions of your visual scent and, when it was ripe, plucked it. It pains me to have employed a similar level of deceit and treachery to that of Lupin's. However, I have done two things that Lupin did not: I have given you as much knowledge as I am able, and I have taken no more than your visibility; your possessions are safe. The life of an Unseen is a despicable existence, but this does not mean one should allow oneself to throw morality into the gutter. It is my hope that you will show similar mercy when the time comes. Take this guide and learn from it. It contains your escape route.

Now all that remains for me to do is apologise with all my heart. I am truly sorry and I wish you well.

A big thank you to Carolyn for helping me hold my shit together for long enough to publish this damn thing. Your editing skills, assistance with the story selection, and your calming influence have been invaluable.

A bunch of other kind souls have helped me in various ways: Lesley and Keith especially, and all the amazing readers who read the 'beta' version and gave feedback. Thank you.

ABOUT THE AUTHOR

Sef Hughes was born in Glasgow, has lived in Edinburgh, Newcastle, Leeds, Pittsburgh, Amsterdam and Eindhoven, and is currently hiding out in a small fishing port on the North Yorkshire Coast. *Salt Water* is his first collection of short fiction.

Find out more at www.sefhughes.com.

Printed in Great Britain
by Amazon

49500399R00121